"Ibáñez-Carrasco introduces us to a vision of the urban queer never glimpsed in advertisements for tight shirts and designer jeans. His is a four-thirty-in-the-morning, done-one-too-many-lines-of-crystal lens. The heroes in his stories can be HIV-positive, not white, and sometimes self-loathing. If you scraped the rainbow paint off your pride rings with a dirty thumbnail, you would find Francisco's world, skillfully rendered and beautifully imperfect."
—Ivan E. Coyote,
**author of *Close to Spider Man* and *One Man's Trash: Stories***

"Francisco Ibáñez-Carrasco is a fine writer. These stories about people on society's margins are both disturbing and moving. Take a look."
—Michael Nava,
**author of the Henry Rios series**

"*Killing Me Softly* introduces a new voice to gay fiction, seductively Latin, Poe-esquely North American, very contemporary, and seemingly utterly unafraid. Ibáñez-Carrasco is someone to watch."
—Felice Picano,
**author of *Dryland's End* and *Fred in Love***

"Francisco Ibáñez-Carrasco's new collection of queer urban stories, *Killing Me Softly: Morir Amando*, should not be called fiction, it's so true. This Last Exit to Vancouver may feel like documentary vignettes of the people you've seen at the gym or on the street corner, but it's also cliff-hangingly melodramatic, bitter but also compassionate—an outsider's unforgiving canvas of the complacent yuppie West Coast of Canada in the new century but also an insider's sentimental register of the pulse of an organism that is throbbingly alive. Ibáñez-Carrasco has a sharp eye, a flaming tongue, and a greedy libido that wouldn't let me put this book down."
—Thomas Waugh,
**author of *The Romance of Transgression in Canada: Sexualities, Nations, Moving Images***

# KILLING ME SOFTLY:
## MORIR AMANDO

FRANCISCO IBANEZ-CARRASCO

# KILLING ME SOFTLY:
# MORIR AMANDO

FRANCISCO IBANEZ-CARRASCO

suspect thoughts press
www.suspectthoughtspress.com

Author photograph by Britt Permien
Cover image and design by Shane Luitjens/Torquere Creative
Book design by Greg Wharton/Suspect Thoughts Press
Print management by Jackie Cuneo/Little Jackie Paper

First Edition: December 2004
ISBN 0-9746388-1-1
10 9 8 7 6 5 4 3 2 1

Library of Congress Cataloging-in-Publication Data

Ibáñez-Carrasco, J. Francisco (Jose Francisco), 1963-
  Killing me softly : morir amando / by Francisco Ibáñez-Carrasco.
    p. cm.
  ISBN 0-9746388-1-1 (pbk.)
  1. Gay men--Fiction.  I. Title.
  PR9199.4.I23K55 2004
  813'.6--dc22

                    2004012636

Suspect Thoughts Press
2215-R Market Street, PMB #544
San Francisco, CA 94114-1612
www.suspectthoughtspress.com

Suspect Thoughts Press is a terrible infant hell-bent to publish challenging, provocative, stimulating, and dangerous books by contemporary authors and poets exploring social, political, queer, spiritual, and sexual themes.

# PUBLICATION CREDITS

Grateful acknowledgment is made to the following print and online publications in which these stories originally appeared in slightly different form:

"Chameleon," *suspect thoughts* (www.suspectthoughts.com) Issue 1, 2000, Greg Wharton, ed. "Hockey Night in Canada," *Arts & Understanding*, October 1996. "Hurt Me, Mi Amor," *Contra/Diction*, Brett Josef Grubisic, ed. (Arsenal Pulp Press, 1998). "Mountain Dew," *Velvet Mafia* (www.velvetmafia.com) Issue 1, 2001, Sean Meriwether and Greg Wharton, eds. "Mr. Deluxe or the Midlife Crisis of Others," *Velvet Mafia* (www.velvetmafia.com) Issue 8, 2003, Sean Meriwether and Greg Wharton, eds. "Spunk," *Of the Flesh*, Greg Wharton, ed. (Suspect Thoughts Press, 2001); *The Mammoth Book of Best New Erotica*, Maxim Jakubowski, ed. (Carroll & Graf Publishers, 2001); and *Law of Desire*, Greg Wharton and Ian Philips, eds. (Alyson Books, 2004). "Strictly Professional," *Best Gay Erotica 2000*, Richard Labonté, ed. (Cleis Press, 1999).

# ACKNOWLEDGMENTS

The craft of writing—a craft like a time-travel capsule—is for me a guilty and secretive habit, sometimes pleasurable, sometimes selfish and vindictive. My friends know this, and they allow me to do it; they inspire passions into these characters. When people ask me whether the characters are true, I sometimes say they are composites, sometimes a pack of lies.

These short stories are calculated little lies because art lies and it allows us only to point fingers at certain things, not others, so you, the audience, can see glimpses of imagination and not the full texture of living (that would only make our heads spin). I thank those who allow me to create art capsules to make living imaginable. First, I must thank a pack of ghosts, *los fantasmas en Chile y Latinoamérica, en los Estados Unidos y en el gran Canadá*, all those ghosts who perished as the band played on. I can hear the rustle of their memories left behind, like breaths of chilling air into the rooms we occupy. And I must thank the ones left behind, those of us, an old guard of gay men living with HIV, strange and tenacious gargoyles, hell-bent on living. May the memory of ghosts give us strength and joy.

And I still squabble with whomever says that my stories are only to be read with one hand by homosexuals or that they are—as someone wrote about my first novel—about illness and a cast of bitter misfit fags, dreary and weighty. They are stories about love; they are about living for love, the love that one may die clutching to one's heaving heart.

More thanks are due, and this time with particular zeal to two men who serendipitously came into my life and dignified my craft: Greg Wharton and Ian Philips, you have taught me something crucial about myself: to be confident and dignified in my words. What angels of merciful quills, what dedicated nurses to a triage of words!

## DEDICATION

Who can say if there is a one and only? Who can make time stand still so it is not shattered like crystal? If there is ever a moment eternal, a minute of one's life, a whisper in one's ear in which the man holding you is the only one, then one must drown in those eyes and live that moment without fear. I dedicate this book to my Johnny Peirson, who brings that moment here every day with amazing generosity of heart. I love you, babe.

# CONTENTS

# STRICTLY PROFESSIONAL

*Is Heaven a physician?*
*They say that He can heal;*
*But medicine posthumous*
*Is unavailable.*
*— Emily Dickinson*

*Mi nombre es España*, well that is not my real name, *es mi apodo, y la historia que les voy a relatar* does not end today, it is, like they say, *el principio de un final feliz, como las canciones*, the songs with happy endings, even when it is my ending. España is my name 'cause my girlfriends, in Cihuatenejo, called me this as I grew up in the beauty salon where my mother worked. They said that I had the *garbo* of the flamenco dancer, *la maja*, la Lolita. They knew I was destined for better and bigger things, for a life of luxuries and softness. The road has not been paved with roses. I say it's more like cobblestones all the way up the West Coast, but in the beginning of the end, the life after living, I am a comfortable heiress to the Hispanic jewels in the crowns of my sovereign ancestors. *Ay niña, que volada que me siento, me voy en fiebre*, pull that chair over, *niña*, and I will tell you a story of how I got to this house, this humble-yet-stylish government-subsidized abode, of how I live the way I do, *debatiendome entre el amor y la morfina...*

A morphine surge tongued me inside out. It takes about sixty seconds for the blood to circulate once through our entire vascular system. The origin of my elation was his hand that thumbed the end of the syringe; a gush ran wild through my veins. I was spiraling and hollering, *Whoop-dee-doo!* I didn't actually utter a sound for the sheer pleasure of suffering in silence. I held on to the stretcher railing as the world turned around and my skin mutated through various shades of pale. He said, "You told me you weren't allergic to morphine." I thought, *I have told you so many things* as I filled up a kidney basin with acidic fluids from my stomach. Then I could hear him behind the curtain say something to a nurse. A lost soul shrieked nearby; it was Halloween and a frantic rhythm reigned in the ER. The nurse sternly responded she couldn't go and help, too many men, too little time. Grudgingly, he came back with another syringe. Ah! Gravol, my favorite. He was not very deft at using the needleless equipment. So what? He would be a doctor and never have to do the menial work again. He stretched my arm—I'd had my hands drawn against my chest as if clutching my pearls—and my hand ended up positioned squarely under his crotch. He was nervous. I had the shakes. A bad combo. The liquid was not getting through so he asked me to pump my hand, "open, close, open, close." He was putting himself through the motions with a very focused whisper as he tried to hold me down on the stretcher. I let myself go like a child on a ride at the fair as the fluid merged swiftly into the maddening traffic of my blood. Once the Gravol completed one entire bodily circuit, I let go of the handrail with a neigh. I lost my other grip on his crotch and fell into an orgasmic stupor thinking about him, the doctor, my doc.

Earlier that night, I had made my way through a packed waiting room where there was a midnight gridlock of intoxicated ghouls and witches, young men in ridiculous muumuus and smutty lingerie. Halloween, the one night of the year in which straight blond boys give free rein to their desires to wear women's clothes and flaunt their femininity. I had psyched myself up for this occasion for a long time, planning every detail, laying out contingency plans, plans where everything was designed to go wrong but not terminally so. It took more than simply watching hospital dramas on TV. Move over divas. ¡A la primera estupida que se me cruze por el camino, la mato! The first time I saw his striking face, he stood out from the other students gathered around the instructor. His eyes were avid and compassionate at the same time. Later, while doing his rounds, he came back to say, "I'll get you through this" (Oh you already did, gorgeous). I knew he was sincere and innocent—both flaws more fatal than ignorance (ever see Fatal Attraction?)—and that he'd never seen much daytime drama. He didn't know the scripts. All the lines sounded fresh to him. He was a catch.

It takes work to be a conniving villain, a seductress victim, an erotic martyr, a caring serial killer, o un despiadado amante. Se toma tiempo morir amando and I'd like to think that I am a bit of every one of those characters, and then some. It is not like my life has been simple, but after years of enduring freakish opportunistic infections, shooting pains, consuming dull aches, and torturous treatments, I am savvy. I know what I am doing. Tengo mas vidas que Susan Lucci's Erica on All My Children. The turning point in my adult life has not been a silly diagnosis; it was meeting him, Mandouh, when I landed in the ER at 2:00 a.m. I fell in love. I learned later that what I had was septicemia; irrelevant indeed. It could have been pneumonia or anything else; all I knew was I was drenched in sweat and delirious. I had called a friend, and he took me to the hospital. I was so sick that I cleared triage in a record time and was spared the admitting process. I was plunked onto a stretcher and wheeled into one of the cubicles. My friend and a chunky practical nurse prepared me as they exchanged "I know which way you swing" looks (would it have killed them to send an RN!). Baring it all at an ER is much like going to those gay saunas. In both, they give you a towel or a gown to pretend you are clean and modest. "There's always so much need and too few good people working in public hospitals, don't you think?" said my friend to the obsequious practical nurse by way of small talk. The LPN batted his silly eyelashes and agreed (I rolled my eyes. *Oh please. Spare me.*). The LPN took all my vitals, awful stats, and wrote them in his chart. Before leaving, he told me that the intern would be along anytime now. In fact, he did not address me; he probably thought I couldn't speak English. As if she could. *Polaca de mierda.*

One hour elapsed during which I let loose all kinds of personal expression. I cried, feeling sorry for myself; I cried in pain, in anger; I yelled and cried some more. I grabbed my good friend's hand and asked him to feed my cat and not to borrow any of my CDs unless I was terminally ill. He got tired of the scene and softly told me he would go get a coffee and come back in half an hour, or so. He left. *Bitch!* That's when *he* appeared amidst the veils, like a 1940s movie star, a chivalrous horseman of the desert, drenched in sweat but victorious, *varonil, impecable y gentil a pesar de la tormenta de arena, la sed del sol salado de cuarenta grados centígrados de fiebre*, he stepped into my tent pitched in the hot desert ready to save (and conquer) this damsel in distress. However, that first night, this prince did not lay with me; he barely touched me with his fingertips. I woke up. An odalisque surrounded by veils, which in fact were the curtains they demurely draw around you when they come to take your clothes off. Someone began cussing at everyone from the adjacent stretcher, but this did not break my spell, and the young healer paid no attention. In a lovely preamble, he introduced himself, Mandouh, the Egyptian prince, and he came so close to my face I thought I could feel his breath on me. It was so inspiring, *me recordó las historias de pirámides y terroristas armados cabalgando en dromedarios*. I cried, but silently this time.

The nurse came in; he told her to inject 5 cc. of morphine right away. A minute later I was drowning in the quicksand of his big almond eyes. My anchor, the grip of his hand, was firm yet warm. I thought he would make a good surgeon. I thought I would let him shred my body into ribbons of flesh and blood and claim victory all over my land. And I thought of the mix of *La Tierra Madre*, *La Virgen de Regla*, *y La Diosa Egipcia Isis*, all combined in one offering body. And I thought...

I woke up later when they took me for X-rays. I tried to understand the technical reasons they were politely giving me, and I nodded in reply. They hung me like a parrot on a trapeze (I couldn't stand on my own), twirled me around, first this way, then the other; I passed out. When I woke up something had changed in me: I didn't care; I wasn't afraid or reluctant; anxiety had abandoned me, and I had abandoned my body to their care, ultimately, *his* care. When they brought me back from the X-ray room, he was there to tell me that I would probably be admitted to the hospital. It was around 6:00 a.m. I would have to wait for the next available bed. I asked him whether he was leaving; he said he wouldn't leave until he made sure I was admitted. He said, "I'll get you through this." He asked me if I was in pain; I nodded yes; he ordered more morphine; and I basked in its calm chemical oasis while he asked me questions: about my ailments, whether I used street drugs, what I did for living, a list of my medications. I purred out my answers. He asked, "What is your 'risk factor'?" Last time a doctor asked me *that* I laughed in his fucking face! How come they couldn't bring themselves to say something as simple (and as good) as "what kind of sex do you have?" so one could respond, *"me cogieron por el rabo"* (*sin condón*). Or they call it "risk category" — what's with that? Let me spell it out for you: I-got-fucked-up-the-ass. This time I bit my tongue and humbly stretched the phrase "a-nal-pe-ne-tra-tion" and he didn't blink once.

It was then that a flash of genius came upon me: I mentioned that two months before I'd had a herpes outbreak in my rectal area. All those safe-sex words have to come in handy at some point or another. In medical situations they love to hear that one has been properly trained in such florid medical jargon. I explained carefully. He pondered. Once I finished he said, "I am afraid I will have to do a rectal check." I fought hard so my grimace wouldn't become a smile. I used to get hours of rectal action before I got so sick that I had to restrict access up that road. Vladimir, the Russian bulimic impeller I was dating at that time, was not impressed. Fortunately he got pretty sick himself soon after my road closure and was not able to do anything else. He was also hell-bent on hanging me in slings to stuff me full of Crisco like a Transylvanian turkey out of Thanksgiving hell. Fisting was never my thing— *¡Joder! Que obsesión que tenemos algunas por lo anal*—but a good deal of traditional fucking and ass-play was always the dish *du jour* on my sexual menu. I did what I could to nourish my appetite. Carlitos, *el truhán de los ojos esmeralda*, had died some years ago, dreadful end, poor thing, *Dios lo tenga en su santo reino*, so much nose candy, so much agitation, so many shiners I got, but I loved him anyway, *quien te quiere te aporrea. Ya sabes niña*, our Latin version of S/M is so very much more romantic. None of this no-deodorant–no-shaving shit. Anyway, all my other regulars gradually became either too dead or too sick to do anything. I played solitaire most of the time with plastic prosthetics that could never replace the moody, yes, overrated, but immensely necessary phallus. *La divina verga*—It is odd that, in spite of its potent patriarchy, *cock* is a feminine word in Spanish. Really strange. But...I digress...back to my story. I remember clearly that the young doc made me roll on my side and that the sound of the latex snapping against his ample palms crowned with strong fingers made me salivate. His voice assured me that it would only take a couple of minutes, to calm down, to relax. *¡Ay papi..que rico fué eso! Me sentí virgen.* This was more than any *maricón* had done for me in a long time, always too hasty to get their fucking rocks off or too fucked up on crystal to get any boner of consequence. It had to be a straight *papi*, naturally, maybe in a clinical way, but such strictly professional relationships (like prostitution) are far more humane and tender than the hurried sex among liberated queers, say I. He gently slid in two thick fingers smeared in cool water-based lubricant (all in absolute accordance with safer-sex guidelines; one can't even get *that* in a one-night stand these days) and glided them around, exploring, asking me what I felt. "Tender?" he asked. "(*Hmm...not really*) Yes, a bit..." He probed a bit farther. "A bit"; he kept on searching. I kept on giving mixed signals, small jolts, a brief trembling, a subtle tightening of my anal muscles; all this interspersed with a few verbal hints. *Ah divina dulzura del pasado y la memoria*, how could one forget the many attentions dispensed to the Chicano boys later in the evenings after casino night, the low riders, too many beers, sudden shots in the air, the shots of tequila, and the shots at me like a punching *piñata*... A huge sigh came out when he withdrew his three fingers. *¿Tres?* I rolled onto my back and pulled the blanket up so he wouldn't see — I hope he didn't see. I might be sick, but I am not dead. Well, if he saw it, he didn't say anything and pretended he didn't — the joy in my eyes. Liberal middle-class professional men can be so respectful and proper about these things. They created the "don't ask, don't tell" to get away with these things. Mandouh, the doctor, concluded that there might be "something up there," but it was hard to tell because I was too agitated. Then came the time to check the rest of my body with his warm hands. He sat me up to check my breathing with the stethoscope, an occasion I used to vomit a bit more, which wasn't too gracious, but I couldn't help it; then he tapped my chest, my stomach, and pressed my groin, and my testicles, and paused to ask me about the lesions on my legs. For a while he ran his hands over them, which was more than the pity or the disgust that I had gotten from the few men I had gone to bed with in the last four years. Men who were so gay, so out, so understanding, but could not get themselves to think about bodies that were not primed, not young and immaculate. But I digress...

He left and came back later with a group of students and the doctor in charge of the ward. They stood around like penguins exchanging little proper nods, lifting the sheet up like in a morgue, poking me, never looking me in the eye. Mandouh stood out in this curious lineup with his tight curly hair, his incredible eyes, probably around twenty-four, if not less, with an impeccable accent and fluoridated teeth, strong neck and nose, and a clean-shaven sharp jaw, surely an exemplary DNA. *Ay no me mires asi niña*, what a look you give me, like this, *mira así, así.* I have never been interested in adolescents, but there was something so wise and mature about this kid. I was his first, his first patient; I became patient for him in true devotion. *Entrega total.* I was *his*; he could determine what was to be done to me, what could happen to me; he could inflict care or pain, delay the time or rush me through another set of questions and tests. And to think that I had wasted my time looking for men in all the wrong places, even thinking that leathermen would be more aggressive, dominant, loving. They turned out to be more often than not racist old white men or young plastic studs who didn't have the first idea about controlling someone or getting a hold of themselves, their holes, their drugs. Often, they wanted to be cruelly fisted, abused, and disposed of before their highs wore off so they could forget about the night and go on with their stupid lives as if nothing had happened. Sound-bite love. Internet roadkill. Until the day they get diagnosed with HIV: shocked, desperate, they start mouthing off about their fucking civil rights and crying over government neglect. They would have a fucking epiphany and shed crocodile tears about AIDS-phobia and sexual discrimination within the self-absorbed gay community while all along they had done all those things in their own private lives. *Ay niña que se desborda el veneno por mis labios como el rocio matutino de una fruta jugosa y maldita.* Vitriolic? *Moi?* Maybe. It's only the drugs that allow me to get naked and sincere, to be *la España que siempre fuí, la de Garcia Lorca.*

It was ironic but not surprising that I would so amorously submit to a heterosexual man with a well-fed body, morals, and authority. Isn't this the secret wish of many AIDS queens? *¿Quien no desea un soldado, un bombero, un carpintero o un médico?* Someone who can alter the course of your life by wielding a sharp or blunt object. To want to be cared for like a wounded animal, precious and fragile, even if his was just a clinical interest, the need to "check," scrutinize, to listen to the murmur of my heart, the croaking of my bowels, the cracking of my bones — to listen attentively to my sexual exploits, which I recounted in detail and with added spice — and remain strictly professional. I prolonged my answers to let him know of the things my body could do, the arching and releasing, the highs, the abandon. I scrutinized him too, looking for a glimpse in his eyes. It took some time but I think got a faint signal, imperceptibly so, the way a man looks at an animal in the zoo and the animal looks back and he wonders who has really trapped whom. That night when the penguins, *los matasanos*, left my cubicle, Mandouh stayed behind writing in his little black notebook, closed it up, remained silent, and slightly squeezed my hand as he was leaving. That gentle squeeze felt like lightning. I was too tired to say or do anything. He didn't say goodbye and good luck.

My friend was there; he had come back from his coffee (with that slut practical nurse, surely) and was mesmerized by this Christian *tableau vivant*, a saint holding a sinner's hand. He is very well educated, so when Mandouh, the Sphinx doctor, left, he was quick to mention that he had seen this same scene in an old Benetton magazine devoted to AIDS a long time ago. *Ah.* And he also added that I should remember what the psychologist I had seen had told me about "transference" or some shit like that, about falling in love with one's caregiver, the way I had initially with him, or was it falling in love with one's torturer? Anyway, he got all hoity-toity for a moment there (charming bitch, ain't she? *¡y la puta que la parió!*). I told him he was jealous. He said he was, but that was not the point; that I had no hope in hell, being an ailing person and all; and that he would have better chances and would let the young doctor have him anytime; in fact he thought he could be gay and that he had made some kind of eye contact with him. *Wishful thinking, honey! You should content yourself with dating the help.* But I said, "I think the orderly was very interested in you." "He's an LPN. You should know better, queen of the sick."

An hour later I was taken to a room on the ninth floor from where I could see the blue velvet of early morning draped over the city, and the fine winter drizzle and lights in the buildings sparkling like diamonds. As the two sublingual Ativan worked their sleep magic on me, I could see Mandouh, the young doctor, tired, getting home to a nice neighborhood, stepping out of a nice, unpretentious car, turning off the lights in the living room that had been left on throughout the night, making his way to the bedroom with a glass of milk in his hand, brushing his gorgeous smile, taking his clothes off almost inaudibly, only a rustling noise as they brush against the soft pelt that covers his tight skin, a noise one can only hear in the movies, revealing his sturdy body, releasing the sweet bitterness of his deep armpits, and lying down next to his blonde girlfriend—How did I know she was white? Pure intuition, I guess—to fall sound asleep, touching her hips for a moment...the tips of my nipples responding as I stretch between our sheets like a lazy cat, and he is dedicating his next tiny thought to me, embracing me without hesitation. Our clock ticks, like the IV dripping into my central line, and slowly puts our thoughts to rest since we both know that everything is all right.

So I starved myself like a Catholic schoolgirl who has fallen in love with her most handsome young teacher. No one could understand what was going wrong with me since the infection that had taken me to the hospital in the first place had been solved, albeit in a rather dramatic way, by inserting a catheter connected to the superior vena cava underneath the clavicle where it stood out under the skin like a little microphone. Now I was bugged. Mandouh could have free access to the intimate contents of my fluttering heart. I was also taking an expensive course of drugs trumpeted as a cure. I was advised over and over again to drink lots of liquids so my kidneys wouldn't suffer and develop stones because the drugs had a high content of calcium. I was told that stones were extremely painful to pass, a pain only comparable to giving birth. (Needless to say, I didn't drink.) And with a bit of strategic phoning around, I found out precious information about Mandouh by way of the Polish LPN my bitch friend had met the first night

I saw Mandouh. My bitch friend was banging the LPN on regular basis now, and he owed me for some party favors. I found out, for example, his schedule. I could not stalk him — that was absurd and kind of psychotic, so *passé* anyway, not really conducive to having someone fall in love — so I decided to approach him on his own turf, nothing too threatening. Straight men are not afraid of queers as long as they keep the illusion alive that they come out on top, or better, that they come out ahead of the game every time. It's not about their fear of anal penetration; it's about their fear of being emotionally taken, compromised, committed, and trapped. I spent some cold evenings in a coffee shop across the street from the hospital (which contributed nicely to my dehydration) checking his ins and outs. After his shift, he was picked up by his girlfriend. As it turned out, she wasn't a curvaceous blonde but sort of a generic, unattractive brunette. She drove a Volvo, by far the most anal-retentive car there is, and dressed quite conventionally, no makeup, and a big Christian fish sign attached to the back bumper (Nice touch. Score one against moi. A big one!). All her little flaws could be points in my favor in some imaginary *Cosmopolitan* personality test. I was in awe of him every time he waited for her. He was tall and wore loose corduroy pants, wool sweaters, and a GAP coat; he moved briskly, holding firmly a brown leather bag, and a stethoscope hanging around his neck. He was a vision even when I wasn't high on drugs (although I am often stoned to endure the pain of chemotherapy and the smorgasbord of other medical procedures I go through weekly). I saw him get in and out of her car a few times, never embracing her but giving her a fleeting kiss (sometimes only on the cheek!). She would smile, he just looked okay, and they didn't burst into conversation or laughter. The dim streetlights at the emergency entrance were great accomplices; they allowed me to observe a bit longer without being seen. After a cold month of adoring espionage—is this what they call a *cordon sanitaire?*—I was ready to see him again, but my health wasn't any worse. I had lost a lot of weight and all my hair, but I looked more butch than ever—and without even trying. I certainly wasn't sick enough to be rushed to the emergency room. It was only by pure serendipity that I learned that there might be a window of opportunity, or better yet, an impending crisis, for me—*serendipity*, I love searching the dictionary for beautiful English words to use on him in my imaginings. In a phone call to a friend who was dying in the hospital, I learned, much to my chagrin, that Mandouh, my Sphinx doctor, had left the emergency room to join the AIDS team on the second-floor ward. The rest of my plan took a bit of sleuthing, but I finessed it quickly. On the night of Halloween, I slashed my wrists. How appropriate. I felt the sibilant caress of the blade, a whisper in my ears, a soft cadence in my legs, and warm blood surging from my veins. Then, I called 911.

My machinations almost backfired: the paramedics, a busty blonde and a beefcake guy, wanted to take me to a different hospital, farther from my neighborhood but less congested with all those fucking goofy heterosexual youngsters who were beating each other senseless in cars and bars on that night of phantoms and ghouls and witches. No way. This would not happen to me. I was on a highly sensitive mission of love, bleeding like nobody's business, and no fucking testosterone-fest would steal the spotlight I needed shining on me! *¡Me volví loca, perdí el control!* I created a scene, and the fuss I made was such: about being taken to that particular hospital because of AIDS, because I always went there every time I was sick, because they had my file...and on and on. The siren outside continued to navigate through the congested city arteries. I was losing blood, I was losing ground, I was tearing the bandages and IV lines inside the rolling cage. I saw red crosses in white fields and corpses driving Porsches and BMWs. I called out racism and homophobia, effective liberal battle chants, until they finally gave up, muttered a curse, told me to be quiet, and took me where I wanted to go and meet my destiny.

In the midst of a masquerade of vampires, skeletons, Batmans, Martians, Marilyn Monroes, and other celebrities, I made my grand hysterical entrance, pulling away at the temporary tourniquet and bandages they had put on me in the ambulance, and clamoring for the grim reaper to come and take me away. They immediately led me into the ER, not into one of the cubicles separated by curtains but into one of the small separate rooms, fast track they call it. This was another lucky break. Like any other suicide attempt, I was bound for the psychiatric ward, but it is so small and there was such pandemonium that they simply wheeled me wherever they could. The guy on the stretcher next to me had a huge blade wound in his thigh. He looked like a whore from the waist down, although the red net stockings weren't his color. A nurse came and tore them open and away unceremoniously, cleaned the wound a bit, put a big patch of gauze over it, and exited, leaving him there all bruised and naked. His sheet had fallen to one side exposing him—*gorgeous*—I took a long hard look at him, which he obviously resented, but was too sedated to do anything about. I said, "I could let you fuck me good, but I'm here to see someone else." He blinked twice, astonished, and fell into a coma or something like that while grabbing at his blanket like a big baby. The next obstacle came after the nurses had bandaged me, hooked me to the IV drip, and taken my vitals: another doctor, no less gorgeous, but looking dangerously like a priest, came to see me and explained in officious words that he would have to report my "situation" to the police stationed in the ER due to "its nature." This was trouble: I didn't want to be committed or anything, far from it. It took me a good ten minutes to explain to him that I was (a) sane (girl) and that I really needed to see an HIV-specialist—whoever was on duty that night (I knew who).

As soon as he stepped into my desert tent, Mandouh recognized me. The beeping of the heart monitor accelerated from "agitated" to "exhilarated." A subtle smile perfected his ample dark face, raising slightly and separating his dark and thick eyebrows. I could smell licorice and cinnamon in the air. Professionally, he asked me what had happened, and the other doctor grabbed him by the arm and took him outside to explain my "situation." When he came back, Mandouh looked serious and asked me to recount what had happened. I told him I was sick and tired of life, AIDS, people's pity, everything; he held my hand and said, "However, you seem in better shape than the last time I saw you." I said, "Thank you. I take good care of myself. I know they have those new drugs. I'm taking them." (You should say that. There is nothing for one's looks like a bit of starvation.) I felt like Maria Callas after her comeback, as slim as a nymph. I used to retain liquid and overeat when smoking pot. I told him right then and there that I loved him—why wait?—but maybe it didn't come out right, maybe it didn't escape my lips at all. He smiled and, I swear, that before I passed out he kissed me on the lips...but I'm not sure.

There isn't much more to tell. I woke up. I was taken care of, I was sent home, but I was able to come back to the hospital where he worked for periodic checkups. It took a lot of work, paperwork and physical work; I put myself through ups and downs, calculated overdoses, weight fluctuations, bouts of euphoria and depression—never too much, never too little, *lo justo y necesario para mantener viva la llama de su científico interés*. My friend—well, ex-friend—got wind of some of this and called me to tell me that I had a serious case of Munchausen syndrome(!). Oh, did she ever get a piece of my mind. *Y la mandé a tomar agua por el culo. ¡Perra!* No one needs friends lacking imagination. How could you label with scientific tags the reasons of the heart? She could still get a bland *Polaco* to bang her sorry ass and make her feel somewhat important. I was under the sweet ministrations of a heavenly physician. He screamed "malingerer" on the phone before I cut her out of my life. Put yourself in my heels, a queen in love with a few options, not like you, fucking gym bunny! But I guess it may sound limited to some, but for me, someone who has a short life expectancy and a narrow range of possibilities, our relationship means a world of difference. Mandouh's life changed; he didn't say that to me, but I once snuck into a public presentation on HIV, and he briefly mentioned how he had come to the hospital to specialize on infectious diseases, and he intended to move on but had found there "a fertile and intriguing field of inquiry" (whatever that means). I felt I had found an opening into vast fields of possibilities. He completed his stint at that hospital, his courses, and graduated. He also got married, and I brought a card to his secretary on the second floor. I'm not sure he got it, but that was unimportant because I could make up for weeks of time apart from him in one single visit. I would squeeze the minutes, slip in my questions about his well-being, and attend to his needs. A doctor is, after all, a doctor, a highly skilled technician. When they are good, they possess a bit of the power of the healer and soothsayer, but surely they are not shrinks. *¿Que sabe nadie de lo que uno lleva dentro?* They might get to see some of the human condition, but that intuition develops over time and only in those who really work with people—some of them are sheltered in stupid repetitive tasks; those are assholes—and Mandouh slowly developed that sixth sense, thanks to me. However, as I was his teacher, I could always slip my motives and my care under his radar. Without many words, gestures, or explanations, I silently followed him through the years. I saw his children grow from a distance, their faces pushed happily against the SUV windows, going on vacations (those times I suffered like withdrawals). He has turned thirty, plays squash twice a week, does grocery shopping on Sundays, visits his in-laws once a month, but in general spends most of his time at work. I see him every week, same place, same time. If I am very sick I go to the hospital; I have a little bag always ready to go: toothbrush, toothpaste, comb, the few things one needs when one is in there. I know the routine. Someone calls the young doctor, and he shows up in the ward. If I am bedridden at home, he sometimes comes over; he politely exchanges a few words with the nurse, the homemaker, the volunteer buddy, or whoever is there reading a magazine—there is not much to do but wait. He closes the bedroom door on his way out after having examined me in private, strictly professional. I fall asleep, tired, with a bittersweet taste in my mouth, like a fairy in a cabbage of crumpled sheets.

It all happened this way, *igualito a como te lo cuento*, as I have told you, step by step. This is how far I have come and how little road I have left to walk to meet my maker. Why would I lie to you? *España* does not lie because, like *la madre patria*, the motherland, I am made of vicissitudes, *esfuerzo*, victory and passion. *Así ocurrió, así fué*, and thus it will be remembered. You should be leaving now; it is almost time for the afternoon rounds.

He ducked to dodge a Crisco-and-shit glob propelled in his direction—a close call. A doubt clouded his jade green eyes, but he remained nonplussed by the hand-balling fallout. Moments later, he tiptoed outside the room thinking of Gordon and of having seen quieter times.

Mr. Deluxe went to their room—it was out-of-bounds for sex, their rule—and lackadaisically combed his red hair before the mirror as he pondered causes and options. He would sit this one out. They could dog each other good for all he cared. The abandon of their sexual guest, a young cub suspended in the sling set up in the living room, made Deluxe reminisce and feel rather frustrated. Having been a destitute orphan didn't mean he should forever roll over and take it, no matter what had gotten into his master's head. Granted, the cub *"du jour"* was a jaw-dropper, but Deluxe understood well how relative age is.

Gordon's pace had fastened in the weeks since his fiftieth birthday; summer had only added brio to his urgent biological metronome. He was the strong silent type, but he used to pamper Deluxe—or D. as he once called him affectionately—more often. D. didn't ask for much, only some TLC. Maybe it was Gordon's diagnosis so late in life that was making him change. Deluxe was not judgmental about infections; he prided himself in having a good grasp of the human psyche.

Events, however, seemed to spiral downward in the following weeks. After putting in long hours hauling luggage on the airport tarmac, Gordon would come back to the apartment, and tired as he was, tired of work and from the pill-induced nausea and vomiting, he would obsess over sex. D. sighed and stretched as if it were none of his business. Pity had never been his strong suit. "You don't care, do you?" Gordon muttered. "As long as you have food to eat." Now jealousy, that *was* D.'s weakness and that very evening his jealousy was stoked when Gordon sprinted to the corner store. D. thought it would finally be a quiet evening shared by the two of them and had waited by the window until he saw Gordon lumbering up the street with a scrubby type in tow — tall, lanky, high military boots, worn-out fatigues, and the greasiest tank top. At the corner, they stopped; they seemed to be negotiating. By the time they got in, D. was sitting on the ripped leather sling, a mischievous glint in his eyes. The evening came to a screeching halt.

An Easter parade of Duracell-manic fuck-bunnies later, Gilberto, the young Brazilian, appeared in their lives. Both Gordon and D.'s first impressions shifted quickly. Although not as young as his predecessors, or as energetic, Gilberto was oddly charming in his wrinkled khakis, scuffed-up loafers, T-shirts with tiny lizards on them, and his scent of curdled cream and cardamom. On one of his visits Gilberto shyly mentioned his "career" in the "health care industry." "Doing what?" spat Gordon dryly. Gilberto hesitated more than usual and whispered in his thick accent, "ER...orderly." Gordon burped and yawned, and so did D. — they could do this on cue — and without further ado Gordon turned Gilberto around by the neck to fuck him again, but the young man resisted. They'd run out of rubbers. Gordon rolled his eyes, withdrew to the bedroom, slapped on some clothes, and took off for the corner store, huffing.

In those few minutes that Gilberto was left alone with D. in the apartment, instead of snorting up what was left of the crystal as all the others would have done, Gilberto picked out an old record from a forgotten stack in a corner of the living room, slightly dusted the turntable, and played a scratchy version of "McArthur Park." Their eyes met as they silently listened to a spinning bit of past glory.

Gordon yanked the needle from the turntable. He'd come back dragging in a squeegee boy and introduced him as "Pete." The kid, barely seventeen, made a beeline for the little mirror and bent over to snort a couple of leftover lines. Gilberto grew sad and left soon after, claiming he had a night shift at the hospital. D. was dismayed. D. had taken a liking to him, but Gordon seemed not to care one way or the other. "He can take a mean ride, this Gilberto boy," he'd said to D. disdainfully. "I'll give him that." But Deluxe knew Gordon, and he'd overhead them having one or two good conversations.

The same night, a Saturday night, after Gilberto had gone and the squeegee boy had climbed up onto the patched-up sling, like a monkey in a tree, Gordon didn't stop bingeing. More nose candy was produced, and on they partied. Gordon got online, sending and receiving messages, exchanging photos of implausible erections and body twisters—among them, a snapshot of D. playing with a gerbil that D. thought was a tad tawdry. At around ten, two king-size Germanic types and a Chihuahua shaking like a vibrator came over. "Shit, there's enough meat on those two to feed that wretched dog better," reflected Deluxe. Gordon checked *the goods*. Tiny. His disappointment was evident. The Germanic boys seemed to want to stay, Gordon was a hot-looking leatherman, the squeegee monkey on the sling could be removed, and D.,...well, who's to judge? They were a couple pussies themselves. Online, they'd said they were tops, but they *all* say that, and Gordon was used to stepping up to the plate. "Uh. Uh. It's the gym drugs," huffed one of them while looking at his endowment with a zigzagging smile. A probation period followed. Five minutes. They couldn't perform, and Gordon sent them packing unceremoniously. At this point the nose candy and an E tablet they had dropped made them peak, and a sort of desperate but loving frenzy galvanized the room. D. decided to maximize his options and dragged out a serious dildo in between his teeth. He sauntered into the living room with a docile expression on his face. Gordon, ever-quick on the uptake, shoved it up the squeegee boy's ass.

It was two in the morning before they realized there was trouble. The dildo had no handle and would not slide out. Gordon got enough presence of mind to swap his leather chaps for 501s and throw a T-shirt over his heavy harness. "We're going to St. Paul's," he declared. D. was pacing, worried, and Gordon kicked him. The squeegee boy smiled idiotically on the couch until Gordon pushed him toward the door. Deluxe had barely a second to act. His master and the smiling boy had almost made it out the door when D. managed to slide past them and with a concerned expression made it clear that he was coming along too. Gordon cussed and slammed the door shut. At the top of the stairs, he tried to kick D. out of the way again; a fateful move. D. grabbed his foot, making all three of them tumble down the stairs. Pete the kid began to laugh hysterically. He was okay, but Gordon and D. were hurt.

Disapproving neighbors peeked out from behind their doors. Symphony, the transgendered manager, appeared, wearing a vintage sourpuss expression, and helped them to the lobby to wait for a taxi. Gordon had D. firmly locked under one arm and Pete under the other; he was fuming. Directions to St. Paul's were tersely given, once they were all jammed into the back seat of the Yellow Cab. In the short ride, D. lost his poise and, as he struggled with Gordon, got caught in the turban of the East Indian driver. The car swerved dangerously a couple of times; there was cussing and a screech; chaos ruled the cab for a minute. Gordon quickly helped the driver disentangle the cloth from his eyes so he could see the road, and he shook D. hard, and he slapped the squeegee boy even harder, but this didn't stop Pete from laughing like a hyena. And on they went, racing down the street. At the ER entrance, Gordon had to tip an extra fifteen dollars to the livid cab driver for a five-dollar ride.

Once inside the hectic ER, they huddled on a dilapidated banquette under the stern gaze of a Nurse Ratched and a burly security guard whose blue uniform was almost bursting at the seams. *Aha!* D. recognized him. It was one of the Germanics. By then, the impaled kid was contorting and moaning so loudly that the burly guard came over, grabbed him by the shoulders, and pushed him down hard on the seat to shut him up. Pete had another orgasm. "My stars! They're horned-up all the time," Deluxe mused. "Why not spade them? It's the sensible thing to do."

When they finally made it through the triage station, the squeegee kid with the implanted hard-on was taken away to be put under and have his pleasure removed. Gordon and D. were sent to Fast-Track where the nurses, much to D.'s amazement, complained about his presence. It took an hour for the night-shift doctor to show up. It was Gilberto! Their interview was awkward, but D.'s eyes widened. He reclined on the stretcher, next to Gordon, looking catatonic, upping the dramatic ante. In terse words, Gilberto and Gordon discussed the injury, but never a word about their previous acquaintance was exchanged—the famed gay code of silence, D. surmised—and then they discussed Deluxe's future as if he weren't in the room. D. was used to this. "I can take care of *my* pussy," sneered Gordon. D. rolled his eyes. "Really?" said Gilberto calmly. "Only if *I* look after your broken ankle." D. blinked twice—their eyes met again and D. saw a flicker in those Brazilian eyes. Gilberto left, but kept returning throughout the night. Still, no painkillers were ordered. It was a showdown. Two hours later, things came to a head. "Can you take it as hard as you give it?" asked Gilberto point-blank. "Try me" was the master's response. "No promises though— you know, nothing ventured..." And so, at the break of dawn, a hard deal was struck, and a nurse came with a shot of Demeral.

For weeks, Deluxe stayed with Gilberto, and they were both visited by Gordon who reported his progress: no more late nights, squeegee boys, or crystal. Gordon shook most of his old habits, except the sling. Then, they shared D.'s custody on the days that Gilberto had to do his residency shifts at St. Paul's. About six months later, the three of them began to share a bed. Mr. Deluxe lived to be twenty, in a spacious apartment near the park. His coat was brushed so frequently that he almost never got hair balls. In his twilight years, he developed a slight addiction to Fancy Feast.

*[Wide angle: a motel bathed in the neon light of a huge number 6. As we pan into one of the windows, through the slight partition in between the curtains we hear the faint sound of Jimmy Scott's voice.]*

He grabs her from the back and brutally slides into her. I moan. His hands keep a firm grasp on her hips and leave imprints, and then they creep up to her firm breasts, so white. My hardened nipples kiss the cold tiles, my back curves in ecstasy, like a bow it readies to shoot an arrow. I moan. He thrusts in and out with the precision of a well-oiled machine; tongue and groove, he digs into my flesh. Then his hands glide again across the deep valley of her smooth and heaving stomach to land in her mound of pubic hair. I moan. And start to grow. I can't help it. He shrieks and recedes, pulls out of her in an instant, leaving me empty, his huge cock oozing in angst, still throbbing. I turn around, and his face in the twilight is a disgruntled mask of horror. He takes two steps back, lets out another shriek. You're a...! What the fuck... How! You. Freak! His big hands are coming toward me; his cock now is limp, shipwrecked. Instead of scurrying, I wrestle and push him hard against the wall, laughing aloud. My fists land on his contorted grimace, and I swiftly kick him out of the motel room — a naked, beautiful, wealthy brat, a college jock, broad shoulders, cropped red hair, a mercenary of lust, no longer inebriated. Suddenly snatched from the spring-break dream, so awake. Startled. Out! Out, I say, into the cold starry northwest night, in the middle of nowhere. While he, panic-stricken, kicks the door. Thirty seconds later he pleads lukewarmly *pleeease*, then yells in rage. Poor cartoon, screaming like a Fred Flintstone, locked out by a prehistoric figure. He's thinking fast but ineffectively about what to do, what to do, what to do, and his poor butt getting colder. Pity. Inside. I look for his wallet, his gold watch, his BMW keys, his license, and his credit cards. I'll ditch them later; it has to look like a robbery, a joy ride. Not that he would tell anyone. Who would? Tell what? Too embarrassing. I get dressed in his gray sweat pants, wrestling team T-shirt, and runners, all a bit too tight to encase my flabby meat, and slump out the back window.

[Cut to: Corporate building, a three-story high erection caressed by a balmy breeze. Minimalist-décor reception desk and stick chairs flank the entrance where a well-poised receptionist with a thin wireless headphone greets us good morning in a clarinet voice.]

Day after day in the mailroom, I look at the agile young man of slender architecture as he walks by in the company of other gorgeous young men or silvery hawklike CEOs or women in little Gucci or Prada numbers. He is slick, Armani, Hugo Boss, not charming; he is arrogant. He barely looks at me with those strange gray eyes, black eyelashes, maybe Eurasian; he must be about twenty-five. When I deliver the mail, the faxes, small courier packages, his hands do not receive; his index finger points, put it there. An impeccably manicured nail. When he is not around I have taken to checking his appointment book; later I fiddle with his Palm Pilot. Not too hard to come up with a pass code — I calculate his age, nine inches cut, and the number of fingers on his hands, add and subtract, and I got it — yup, predictable. No one would suspect that the moron-looking, middle-aged, plump mailroom guy could work that one out (or any piece of technology for that matter). I say, never trust an ugly face. I find out he is on his way up the corporate ladder, his dates with several women scheduled like business meetings. He meets older women, high-end managers. I can tell by the small gifts he purchases and by the gifts they give him. He is fucking his way up the ladders and snakes, moving and shaking, only enough shaking; he reminds himself of the perfumes they like; he memoes himself about the conversations that are successful, selected lines, the restaurants they like, the number of orgasms they fake, and small budgetary annotations; thrifty fellow he is, strategic to the max. I find out and memorize numbers, domicile, directions, and identifications. I repeat the numbers like incantations. I begin to sweat, and I smell foully; "mendacity," Tennessee once wrote in a play, mendacity. I have to pause; I turn the little gadget off and sneak out of the well-appointed office and hurry back to my fluorescent lair in the basement.

I pull my hair steadily—it hurts—and I pull harder until it has loosened about ten inches. Ain't that different from the operations that those upstart mini-supermodels have to go through, right? I collapse onto a decrepit sofa— cheap room and board—my hair is thinning; it hangs lovely, straight; later I will shampoo it with a temporary sienna reddish tint that he will recognize because I know it is the hue he prefers; small amounts of money he will never notice have gone missing from one of the many company checking accounts he oversees. Later I will use hot wax, which exquisitely excoriates my skin, leaving it smooth and sensitive to the slightest touch. I read *In Style* and *Vogue* and *Cosmopolitan* and about the lives of serial killers. I answer personality tests; examine culinary tips, aromatherapy, pheromones, aphrodisiacs, etc. I follow all the romantic arrangements methodically. It's a long weekend. With my thick hands I grab my chest and pull on my skin until it caves under the pressure, forming two large breasts. I polish their ends into two alert round nubs that will barely insinuate themselves under a thin, light moss green velvet blouse casually thrown over a demure dark-wine-colored medium-length skirt *à la* Julia Roberts. I massage my neck, my hands, my buttocks, my legs, and my feet for hours, refining them, until they have adopted the desired silhouette, the enticing curvaceous lines. The day rolls on sluggishly, and I am anointed by the purring of Billie Holiday; a day of frugal eating; only grapes and drops of water give my skin the complexion and the paleness I know he finds desirable, that anorexic heroin-chic look he falls for — Uma Thurman, Nicole Kidman, Gwyneth Paltrow, Jewel — girls he adores; petals. Finally, I am ready for the conclusive touch. The suffering is excruciating as I press hard, with all my might, on my cock with one hand, on my Adam's apple with the other, inward into my skin, past the bones, until they are absorbed into my body, a process only soothed by my acidic tears. I am now complete: my voice is that of Kathleen Turner and Lauren Bacall; my eyes are not red anymore; my eyelashes luscious, my cheeks exquisite; my tears have evaporated into a subtle perfume of roses, old-fashioned yet not overwhelming, a scent that will surely cast a subtle veil over the senses of anyone who draws near.

*[Close in on a renovated heritage house in a narrow street, quiet, under a roof of magnolia trees sweetly rocked by a slight breeze. A clicking of high heels approaches gently from the end of the street; a cab speeds away; a cat purrs on a nearby branch; two shapely legs walk up to the house; the living room light is on.]*

It's late spring; evenings can be cool, deceiving; evenings can be dark. But I soon take shelter on his front porch, quickly knock at his door; no one else in sight. Slightly agitated, he opens it, wearing dark pleated dress pants, dry-cleaned and pressed to perfection, no shirt, a compact triangle of ribbed muscles gets lost behind his leather belt that hangs undone. He is to meet with some midlevel woman manager; I know, my timing is perfect. My eyes widen with a hint of fear; I utter a nondescript little sound; I deliver a heavenly mirage. I'm sorry, I say; he says, May I help you? I'm sorry, I barely pronounce. My eyes shy away. I begin to turn around to go back down the flight of stairs and exit from his life forevermore. He can see my petite waist, my slender calves, and the thin nape of my neck: damsel in distress, illuminated by the sepia light of the Chinese lanterns hanging on his porch. I barely pause to face him again. I didn't mean to bother you, I say in a whisper that belongs to the rustling of leaves. But I was wondering if I might inconvenience you to call the police for me, 911 actually. Well-intoned lines; Blanche DuBois' revenge; I will not be taken for granted. Is everything all right? he says. I know I'm becoming an intriguing apparition under the pallid spring moon. Confidently, I explain to him who I am, where I work, about my co-worker, who lives down the road, maybe a few houses that way, no, that way, anyway, what's the use, it's so late now, and he invited me for drinks, but when I got there, there was no wife and—I pause to let my eyes well up—it was awful—my tone is buried in a sigh—he wanted more. He looks at me, like the lord of the manor, and says with unveiled smugness that he thought that neighbor was gay, the one from three houses down. I say, So did I, but he tried to force himself on me anyway. My voice breaks like a small wave; I can't go on; I choke up. My car won't start. I show him the BMW keys. I'm standing now in his well-lit mudroom. My hand trembles a bit, fumbling for the dimmer, but he has turned to rush upstairs to his bedroom to put on a well-pressed white shirt. By the time he returns, I am demurely sitting on a stool in his ample kitchen, my legs crossed, showing off their alabaster tone; the heels of my Louis Vuitton black satin mules are soiled with dirt from the grass outside. He seems a bit startled, but he recovers quickly after eyeing my legs. He creeps up next to my handkerchief as it collects a tear from the side of my well-lined eyes. He pours me a tumbler of ice water from the automatic dispenser. I sit, my supple derriere pressed against the soft brown suede of the stool.

A spring interlude, some Debussy, sensible meals, Jenny, Martha, Oprah—blessed be the many goddesses of good living—clean-cut love-making (missionary style, initially, hardly a sigh, a tremolo, the beginning of a lot of learning, unquestioned, unwrapping him layer by layer, imperceptible abrasions on the skin, with restrained drama, without extravagance because I wasn't just anyone). Hulk meets M Butterfly, and the boy captured between these potent icons, this young upcoming corporate man-star, is showered with juices like superstar-named perfumes, a little whiff can make you deliriously mad. I was an affable young lady friend at first, maybe a bit too shy in the light of day, a bit too shy in dimmer light, but I made up for my girlish skittishness with my fascination for the potency of his Porsche's chassis, the reflecting chromium accessories that can be so perversely sensual and cold to the touch of the flesh, and with my fascination for his formidable chest, barren of all primeval hair, glistening only with essential oils, the result of his insistence on ingesting hormones for toning his body, for eliminating fatty tissue, for lies, lies, telling each other sweet little lies, the stuff of millennial courtship. The fact is that he was left spent every night, but greedy as males are, he would come around for more, his eyes eclipsed, finding me like one finds a little orphan columbine in a nest, vulnerable to any contact. Actually, I always came to him, told him how my ex-boyfriend had gone mad, how he was stalking me; I showed him his notes asking for the car he had given me back; a carefully typed "I will not tell anyone about us." I cried, See how he denies my existence and what happened between the two of us, those cherished times; no, don't pick me up at home; I'm sure he's around, watching me; I'll see you this evening. He would hang up the phone with a smirk; happy to bail me out, to help me so he could help himself to me that very same night. Out of the corner of my eye, I could see him shifting his cock under his pants while I sat across the corridor stuffing shit into envelopes of recycled paper and soy-based ink. An easy local call.

I drained every ounce of his anxiety; he was grateful. I intruded into his dreams like sinister metastases. He was cautious at first, but like the good rock climber on sterile indoor walls that he was, he was strong and adventurous. He yielded to my challenges. In the summer he would go back to windsurfing, he said; now he was happy to explore the backcountry. There are so many urges that taunt today's man; life is so fraught with dangerous desires. I smiled as he slowly let go: of his hands; his selfish thick lips; his pristine teeth; his tongue; his words; his lukewarm saliva; the misty suburban memories of his life, all that we learn to describe as repressed childhood memories of abuse and juvenile ambitions; his wallet; his apartment keys; his car keys. I taught him secrets, intimacy, to give in, to trust. I should know well that shattered dreams, crashed vehicles, and charred intentions take fabulous shapes behind closed eyes. It's all about timing, lighting, location, location, location. I initiated him into the perverse secret of my flower, the poisonous vibrations of its raging petals that can stay erect on their stems for hours. A full-bodied flower, protected by thorns that gently scratch his back until it bleeds, just barely, his wrists bound, his legs spread apart until they are slightly strained, my lips careening and descending into every accented curve, a car traveling in the dark of the night, with its high beams on, radiant, dazzling, seeking its destiny, taking each curve faster, harder, longer, deeper, blinder. Our race can only get more sensual, our engines roar harder, the cocaine racing up our nostrils leaving a suave scent of blood, until one night, the car is so hungry for the road, the rubber caresses the glistening pavement with so much passion that it skids, it goes slightly off course, maybe there is another vehicle rapidly advancing from the opposite direction, but we hold on to the steering wheel, I scream, the wheels screech, he moans and heaves, and we swerve and end up by the side of the road soaked in that strange early morning summer light, the window wide open, a breeze blowing through it, through my lips, fluttering like hummingbird wings, his back tensed, his hands trapped in the wreck, his eyes blindfolded, his mouth gagged, his ears covered, moaning deliciously like the precious male animal that he was, that he is, and I could no longer hold the shape of Barbara Stanwyck, I would not be killed in this '40s Hollywood accident, and I end up inside him bursting like the new sun that is advancing along with the emergency lights and sirens. He screams.

*[Cut to: Inside a genteel period house in a shaded street.]*

I say, you will kill for me; he says he doesn't understand her. He says that he will not drink what he drank last night and the night before and the night before, that it gave him nightmares, a bad headache, that he felt strange. How strange? I ask. He says he'd rather not do what we did; it hurts. He does not say where. He is well sheathed in his seamless Calvin Klein's. How good is it? I ask. He is befuddled. Good? He doesn't want to understand. For the time being, we have more important things to occupy our minds: his life crisis; leaving that silly career job; getting more fat onto his body; beer and fries; getting used to the sudden swings in my mood and the inflections in my voice; my late-night vanishings that leave him alone in bed, wanting more, puzzled and in pain; we have to deal with the eviction notice slid under the front door, the concerned calls from cutthroat colleagues, ex-girlfriends, and faraway American relatives.

One day he says he doesn't know how it's all happened, that everything seems to be tumbling down...but she's in his life and that's all that matters, he knows that he loves her, that he wants to lose himself in her, kneel down in front of her, keel over, his eyes uncovered to see the things she does to him, how she tattoos bluish graffiti on his body. The iron doors that barricaded this sanctuary have swung open, drums resounding in the sky of my soul, and the feelings imprisoned inside now overflow. He says he would do anything for her. I say, just wait until you get away from this neighborhood, until you come to my house, no, you've never seen it, I seem to be here all the time, that's right, all the time, wait then, you say you would do anything for me, wait. In front of his eyes, eyes almost coming out of their sockets, I return to my original shape.

In my long life of foster homes, petty crimes, convenience store holdups, runaways, screeching old tires on the greasy pavement of roadside gas stations, I scurried from trailer park to trailer park like an itinerant freak show of one, eating roadkill, never letting anyone see the real me: so whimsical, so damaging. Since I was a child I've been looking for God, but there is no God for those like me, and I understood I had to create my own. So I came, not looking for Mister Right, just looking for the right one for me. I couldn't let the police — social services, the scientists, the counselors — get near me. When any came too close for comfort, I'd disappear and go and settle in new squalor, then amble around the fancy area of town with its towers and the wall-to-wall fantasy, do my little fact-finding missions, and proceed with extreme caution, handle with care, always sheltered by shadows. Shady identities I created, ghouls lifted right out of those B-movies I'd watch late into the morning (I don't need to sleep much). I did underpaid menial work, until I found the next suitor, always hoping this would be the one. A long life of emotional mobility, transience, and instability — as a psychiatric case study would note. One by one I faced the many disappointments. A personal trainer in an uptown gym with expansive hands crowned with ten killer fingers, a roller coaster of bulging muscles with foot odor (I excused that), and a small member (I excused that, too — it's not that I wanted children). He had a voracious appetite for the kinky; there was my hook. But no one is as twisted as they like to believe. That is why they watch movies, to compensate for what they won't dare do — too hesitant, too envious — even in their fucking fantasies. Or the dutiful middle-class father, *Fatal Attraction*'s victim, still so gullible after so many years of horror tabloid headlines, ready to fuck the babysitter at the mere sight of her small-cup bra. (Don't affluent businessmen read *The National Enquirer*?) Or the police chief in his early fifties who would eventually introduce me to his half sisters, half his age, whom he fucked avidly. (The sweetest perversions are tailored and seamed into the staunchest uniforms!) They became an acquiescent audience one sultry evening in a '60s motel room; like two mesmerized owls they witnessed me, perched on top of him, something grotesque and alive, drying breasts, immersed in the sweet agony of metamorphosis that would yield no butterfly out of its cocoon but another worm, bigger and better, *Aliens*, the umpteenth sequel, an improved "Me" in neon fucking lights pumping meat into this venerable patriarch, keeper of law and order, his generous sweat covering his heroic and medalled chest and his glistening ample forehead, as he begged his women for forgiveness, panting hard, and I completed my ferocious ramming of his ass while his women cried, a Greek chorus to his futile tragedy. Stories like these cluttered my life before he came along — like all the men I loved before, big and strong, like songs, like clichés, like long drawn-out puffs of smoke.

But men, they say, are like buses: they come every fifteen minutes (at least if you're in the city); they pick you up and along you go with them, only to get off at your most convenient stop. Tired of the house in the shade of the magnolia trees, the number of distressed calls from friends and family, the number of people who have seen way too many reruns of *Silence of the Lambs*, I needed to move on myself. So I called the red-haired jock: Fine, I'll give you back your fucking BMW, and I'll stop threatening to send an anonymous letter to the bride-to-be, she is indeed lovely, but barren...yeah, I saw the gynecologist's report...never mind how...fuck, I've almost been inside her fucking cunt! Got pen and paper? You got something out of college after all, pretty boy. Did I mention you tasted positively good? A jawbreaker that crazy piece of yours is. No, I said *tasted*, as in your oozing precum, not *tested* as in HIV-positive. Please, don't gag. Write this address down. Hey, you'll get to meet the new improved me in neon fucking lights... *Click.* How rude!

I dance lewdly for him to a cheap '80s punk song, endless love, each night the last, spirits rise, late into the morning light, every day a beginning. It's a lap dance, and the dance is unrehearsed; a little stream of beer flows from the end of his lips, through his rough beard to his gut. The monumental energy in his thirty-something body helps him lift me off the floor to shove his cock inside me, lifts me like a huge crane that crashes against a brick wall, again and again until a gush of fermented liquid empties inside me. I had to teach you so much, my puppy love. Now you love me for what I am, a bit of this and a bit of that.

*[Cut to: Second unit, a large nervous hand grips the front doorknob and turns it quietly. The door creaks open and dim light comes from inside the house. We see tentative footsteps entering the shaded house.]*

Good boy. Not as young as I remembered him. The red-haired jock from the southern team whom I tossed out of a Motel 6 room looks a bit thicker, a bit less surefooted, a bit startled. That's the way I like them! A man is having his way with me. There is blood from somewhere on the gray area rug that covers a portion of the hall. My heels dig into his shoulders, but this butterfly is pinned down real good. Trust the long dicks of men and their short memory: the red-haired jock—just as he did that first night on the highway, when he saved me from the maniacal pastor who wanted to rape me and then took me to a Motel 6 to recover—he now charges my assaulting intruder, the Eurasian man plunging inside me with a vengeance. The jock tries to separate us. All he wants his precious BMW. I doubt he has been able to explain its disappearance or report it to the police. My Eurasian does not let go. Huffing and pounding, his suit pants have crumpled beneath his hips; he's drenched in sweat; his white shirt is stained with my MAC lipstick; and his jacket is coming undone at the seams. He rolled in like thunder this evening, frustrated, almost aware of what his life has become with me, after having been turned down today from a job he was overqualified for.

What is the red-haired jock doing? Why isn't he tearing him apart? I am the damsel in distress who does not scream or flail; I recoil; I tense; but the Eurasian cock inside me keeps drilling. He has squirted all his pent-up juice inside me; I can feel its lubricating warmth. But this is not about breeding: it is about grinding until I shift into my crude daily shape, until he can see me change and kill me. It takes supernatural strength to stay as I am, and I dig my claws into his shoulders, round and muscular under the white shirt, until they anchor in something close to the collarbone. *Thump!* There is one dry and precise thump, and the full inert lips of my assailant come to rest close to mine, so close that a thin warm line of blood trickles into my grimace. His cock is now forever hard inside of me; I slide from underneath him and grasp what is left of my satin nightgown with my trembling hands, covering my breasts. Now my back rests against the staircase's newel; I am heaving, and the red-haired jock stands tall; by his side he clutches a bloodied bottle that is now cut in half and jagged; his jeans are bulging.

I cry inconsolably. I point with a quivering finger to the BMW keys on the lovely hall table. Sobbing, I explain that my attacker was driving a BMW along the highway; I had an engine problem and my cellphone could not get a signal. The monster picked me up and told me that he could give me a ride to my place. We had locked my car and left it on the shoulder of the road. We came here, and on our way he used his cellphone to make a call. He called someone. Called you? I should have stayed there, but it was dark and desolate.

Red seems to want to move and do something stupid (more stupid than I expected). No. Don't call the police. Look! You will have so much to explain. You have saved my life from this monster. The jock makes gestures that he will move nonetheless. How come he called you? Did you know him? He drops the broken bottle; at least he has had the wherewithal to close the front door behind him. He falls to his knees and cries. I will wait a few moments before I console him. The air is ripe with the aroma of Southern Comfort decanting on the floor.

*[Cut to a high wide angle of the two kneeling characters facing each other in silence and a still body face down in a pool of blood between them. They are bathed in dim hallway lights as the camera very slowly glides up the stairs and fades to black.]*

*Now that I have time to reflect on the past years and how I became a successful family man and businessman, I can see all the signs. It started on the day of the wedding.*

Emilia looked radiant that day. Someone remarked that her face was like porcelain; like a Kabuki mask, someone whispered. In turn, someone elbowed that someone and muttered, "She isn't a Jap. She's a Chink, ya goof!"

Dressed in absolute white, Emilia looked serene and acquiescent. Later, like an orchid set ablaze, she enfolded herself into a crimson satin *Kwa* with dragon and phoenix jewelry.

The hall was a nine-ring circus, all day. A small army of local designers had scattered their monikers all over the place. There were the Lees, the Wongs, the Leungs, and the Ngs. They came from the West Coast, the Mainland, Hong Kong, and even Peru. It was a hodgepodge of families whose relation to each other not even the hosts could ascertain. There was a sprinkle of others, from the cellular communications firm where Kevin worked, and jocks from his hockey team, and old high school classmates.

Sneers came from a group of guys in too-tight rental tuxedoes, evidently discontented about having to miss a playoff for a hastily imposed lucky wedding day, as they slurped up the sweet red-bean-and-lotus-seed soup. Emilia demanded that some lucky numbers be observed, numbers given to her by a feng shui expert in her native land. The number eight for good luck, the number three for maternity, and especially, the number nine, which figured prominently in the address of the sizeable house Kevin had bought in Richmond. Kevin's mother had managed to relinquish control on this point and concurred with her new daughter-in-law on the importance of numbers. The tiny, adipose, and chatty Mrs. Ho, one of the members of Kevin's father's family, pointed out with glee that nine would be the number of children Emilia would bring into the world. The newlyweds cracked a smile.

A small army of bridesmaids had donned big hair, as it can only be pompadoured in suburban beauty parlors. The Hong Kong side of Kevin's family wore Donna Karan and Armani, in fairly stiff fabrics, and had soot black bobs.

A rumor set tongues awagging in the hall: everyone desired the luck of the Chinese mail-order bride, but, Kevin—the spoiled brat—had to go and get himself "an import."

And there was music! Many a guest waltzed around, and later in the evening, the drunken ones attempted to dance to the unavoidable "Kung Fu Fighting." The place glittered; there were even clouds of coco-puffs in the ladies' room where petite dresses that had been ordered from fussy seamstresses two months in advance were displayed. And there was enough garish icing on the cakes to trigger a mass outbreak of diabetes. A series of camera flashes worked everyone into a tizzy of splashy cameos for the local society pages that would be accompanied by captions in characters no one from the younger generations could read very well anymore.

That season, Emilia went into hibernation like an orchid in a conservatory.

Kevin went about business as usual. He worked. And after work, he still made time to keep buff, meeting the boys for a hockey game every two weeks and hitting the gym after five, elbowing his way through panting and phosphorescent crowds of bulimic child girls and plucked and hormonally enhanced men. People wrapped in microfibers, raging against the machines, checking their pulse, hoisting themselves into titanium contraptions, carting weights, breaking a brittle nail or two, and baking under the ultraviolet rays of the tanning beds because fungi seem to spread quickly due to Vancouver's eternal dampness. (Vancouver can be odious to the skin in wintertime.) What's more, Kevin was able to make it home in time to share some noodles, kiss the twins goodnight, and retire to his private study, up and up the winding stairs to the end of the hall, and make some necessary phone calls and emails.

He always wore Endurable Tilleys and looked like a tourist, a serial killer, or a pedophile. He had a rare talent for blending in, the way grayish industrial carpet hides bloodstains, vomit, or ink. He also had a talent for spinning a weird yarn when chatting up strangers. Being so unsettling to the ear and the eye, one could not ignore him easily. He had tales of how he'd once been "a somebody," of what he'd read and written, and taught, of his parents being long-faded aristocrats from some Eastern European country. He said that he did not fear falling elevators. This last reference always spooked his interlocutors — it now gave Kevin a discomforting shiver. Kevin felt pinned down by his own stilted politeness as he shared a table in a crowded midday café with this stranger. Kevin's one relief was that this odd man didn't look like he was strung out on drugs — he would have recognized the signs. He noticed out of the corner of his eye that a few colleagues from a rival firm had just sat down a few tables away. He made a quick motion to stand up to leave, but the stranger blurted out what a "supple ass" he had "for an Oriental" in a loud vicious-tongued, yellow-teethed voice. "I am fond of computers too," was the man's non sequitur. Kevin huffed, and for a moment it looked like he would reach over and swat the stranger across the face. Calmly, the man produced a nondescript card from his all-season jacket, and handed it to the crisply turned-out young businessman who instinctively pocketed it before storming off.

*It wasn't until seven-thirty that afternoon, while I was getting it on, that I realized that I had left my cell behind — but where? I dressed in a hurry, oblivious to the whiny blonde who barely creased the hotel sheets — what was her name? Beverly or something. Too bad. I was really getting into it, albeit grimacing a bit, a slight strain leftover from my last hockey game, a real good one.*

Kevin's first reaction was to page his own cell, but he remembered that he had taken to the habit of setting it on "vibrate" to avoid annoying his bosses at the firm during meetings — older people didn't always appreciate the virtue of accelerated communication along with the programmable hockey playoff themes instead of a conventional ring. He called home hoping that one of his five-year-old girls would pick up. Emilia wouldn't answer as she would be pottering around the large kitchen, aloof to any of this, fully focused on food preparation, floating from the counters to the island to the stove, almost ethereally, using her many kitchen gadgets with an uncanny dexterity for someone not always able to read the instructions — unless they were presented in characters.

The new nanny picked up, and painstakingly enunciated that the twins were upstairs. Kevin grunted, in broken Chinese, whether she was able to speak any English. The soft voice fumbled. "Fuck, that's all I needed." And the soft voice on the other side said, "There is no need for that kind of language, sir," in a flawless British accent. He blinked twice, recovered quickly, and ordered her to conduct a full search for a slim, chromium-face-plated, state-of-the-art cellphone. All over the house, except his office, pronto!

He hung up and tried to mentally retrace his steps for the whole day. The flimsy bitch kept pawing him, and the unnatural hard-on from the magic blue pill did not want to wear off. He grabbed the blonde head and shoved it down on him. *Work it fast, bitch. Got to go find my cell.* He bent over the little mirror by the night table and cleaned a line up with one snort.

In September 1993, Emilia had become pregnant. It had taken her three years to conceive; no matter how much roast suckling pig was consumed at the wedding banquet or how many children were allowed to frolic in their nuptial bed. The day that Dr. Pang called Kevin at his office to deliver the joyous news, Kevin told him he'd just received news of a possible job promotion.

That night, Kevin came home later than usual, slamming the portentous front door on his way in. This would be his last day at hockey practice, he announced while fumbling around frantically in the spacious freezer, searching for a bag of frozen peas to soothe a swollen black eye, a shoulder bent out of shape, and several bruises. He barked to the new housekeeper that from now on, he would be eating earlier on the three days he formerly used to go to hockey practice. He ordered her to translate this edict to his wife. He would still go to the gym; he added this as if he were thinking aloud and not really addressing the docile servant.

He turned away to lick his wounds, complaining about "lousy high school classmates, spiteful wannabes, and other bitter assholes." "Three years of my fucking life. I gave three years of my fucking life," he grumbled. "And he had to go and do this to me on this fucking day." He lumbered to the stairs and on his way across the hall, Kevin caught a glimpse of his figure in the full-length mirror. The reflection showed his muscled arm holding the bag of frozen peas against the side of his good-looking face, his buzz haircut, his impeccable teeth, and a streak of blood from his lower lip. In the background, the reflection also caught sight of Emilia watching him. She was standing still in the doorway to the kitchen.

*From that day on I worked so hard to make it, to make it good, for me and my family, to succeed. I did well, but there was always a glass ceiling, one more hurdle I did not seem to be able to negotiate. It was as if I needed to find a genie in a bottle that would offer to make one wish come true.*

That night Kevin made an effort at mounting Emilia that was fiercely resisted. He slapped, forced, and spat, but after a struggle she ran away from the room, barely dressed, ran away from the house with her slippers on, and ran down the street, to reappear only hours later, far away. The police had found her wandering along a highway, dazed but unharmed. They recognized her from her husband's description: a withdrawn, mildly depressed housewife, and unable to speak English. In the months that followed, Emilia became even more distant. The birth of the twins seemed like an afterthought to her in spite of the considerable celebration staged by Kevin's parents. She did not show up often at Kevin's business dinners or even at family gatherings, but Kevin carried her photo and the photos of the newborn twins wherever he went. He kept them as wallpaper for his laptops, framed over his desk at the office, on his locker at the gym, and in his wallet.

Kevin had gone back to the gym where he'd been at five—it was almost nine and the frantic activity was winding down. The buxom instructor—again, a blonde—helped him comb the floors, but they found nothing. She was very solicitous, inspired perhaps by Kevin's unfaltering hard-on.

*I was searching for my cell everywhere. I might have been on my alternate cell for two hours trying to do some potential damage control. I was hurting too; I'd probably taken too much of that pill, and my hard-on wouldn't budge. I made sure I conveyed to Dolores, my assistant, that very important numbers were stored in it. I'd called her at home—she gets paid well. I ordered her to cancel all my credit cards. Yes, some of the numbers were stored on the cell, encrypted, with passwords, but there is always a slight chance. She got on my nerves, wanting to know if I knew any of the numbers by heart. Doesn't anyone follow instructions without asking too many questions? The trainer was almost biting me. I had to stop her with a silent signal. I mouthed the words without sound, "Careful with the Prada. Shhh. Yes. Keep sucking." "Yes, Dolores, some of the card numbers might have been on it." "Just get me off." She looked up at me like I was speaking freaking Esperanto. I forgot she was Polish. Doesn't anyone speak English anymore? "Yes, Dolores, that would be great if you could do that for me as soon as possible. Yes, tonight, for example!" "Just get me off!" That was audible. Dolores, on the other end of the line, shrieked, "What!" And at that precise second I shot and stammered, "Uh...I mean...I need to get off the line." And I hung up.*

He was really starting to obsess about the cellphone. There was too much important information contained in such a small device. The blonde had bolted to hit the shower, and he'd fallen into a soft chair. He huffed as he pulled off his designer's pants, checking for blemishes. He took out his wallet again to check for other 1-800, twenty-four-hour emergency numbers that might need to be called. The stranger's business card fell from his Prada pocket—"Photography and digital services" and an address in a poor suburb some forty-five minutes across the Port Man's Bridge. The card had a couple of handwritten lines on the back. Directions.

*I called the number on the card immediately. Another cell number, of course. The stranger lived deep in the suburbs, far from downtown. It would be a long drive in sleeting rain, but he had my cellphone; no, he had not turned it on, he said. No, he could not courier it, no cash; no, tomorrow he wasn't coming downtown. Not until who knows when. I remember he muttered something about everybody having a life, and added something about rude Chinese businessmen — the drone of his voice transformed the offensive lines into a spell. I was livid but had to keep my cool, take down the directions to a trailer park, make a note to bring a six-pack of Molson Dry and a pack of menthol Craven A.*

Kevin chose to walk down to the trailer park — his Jaguar might get dinged on that potholed gravel road — and after ambling for five minutes he located #7, a trailer home rising out of the midst of the fog, the last in a dilapidated row, some of them boarded up, all surrounded by lanky trees trickling with muted rain. Kevin checked the digital glow on his TAG and cleared his right nostril with the left index finger, again. He got a chill; it was almost ten. The first thing out of the stranger's mouth was a question about his not carrying an umbrella like all Chinese to avoid the sun or the rain. He posed it as innocently as a neighbor who says casually, "Good day, how are you?" Dryly, Kevin demanded his cellphone. The stranger, still dressed in Endurables, waved him in and turned around, leaving the door ajar. Inside, it was hot and humid, the air suffused with something foul, like cat urine, that cheap motel-like polyester curtains trap inside. The large rectangular room was chock full of whirring towers, monitors, gadgets, and a vine of cords. There was a door to a back room and a kitchenette wedged into the wall. Every machine buzzed like electronic hummingbirds, hovering in the rarefied oxygen. Kevin's dilated pupils scanned the room and came to rest on the stranger's pasty figure sitting on a grungy computer chair, his tongue kind of sticking out between a sardonic crack in his thin pale lips, sweat drops, like oil, splattered across his forehead. His long and limp member, like a sleeping maggot, was hanging out of his Endurables. Quickly, Kevin cursed, recognizing his cell carefully lined up with other cellphones on a shelf, snatched it up, and turned to leave, threatening to call the police under his breath, but he was stopped dead in his tracks.

*Not sure how to explain why I continue to do this: visit this back room in my otherwise settled and peaceful life. There seems to be no passing of seasons in this trailer in the lifeless woods; everything remains uncertain yet fixed. Most times, I get there, close the front door behind me, and my lungs begin to fill with the foul air. I take my clothes off and pile them in a corner under the impassive stare of the many blue eyes of the monitors that bleach my skin with their queasy light. I follow precise instructions. I can do this. I excel at work; I am about to break away from the company to launch my own. I have followed his grim instructions to the tee. I kneel down and start working on him, with my tongue first, looking up at his face lording over me, then eating him up slowly, but not too slowly. Often, his acidic taste makes me gag and, like a cat, I arch my back trying to get rid of it all. If I lose it, I'll have to eat it up. I fight hard not to hurl. He clicks and clicks, reruns of sci-fi, working his way up to the snuff. His right hand guides me back down, and I am smeared in my own bile — nose, tongue, and face, all soiled — and a faint feeling comes over me. If I pass out or flail in my own grime, I clean it up in a motel on my way back. I rent a room for an hour to shower and scrub myself until I am nearly bleeding. I repeat these knee-jerk procedures like a bad stutterer; it is like buying and selling stock, getting those last-minute calls, heads-up, indicators, predictions before the Asian markets open. I repeat one enema after the other, before and after visiting him. I don't go there often, only a few hours pass really, only a few weeks pass before*

*I have to show up again, but when I am there it seems like an eternity. I slouch, and kneel, or sometimes bend over into various positions – the gym keeps me limber – and to conclude each session I slowly fit my cellphone into my rectum, which I have smeared with Crisco. He chuckles hoarsely, a couple of times, if I squint and moan too much. I have the flat kind of cell now, without the slip up cover. Once it is inside, I sit in a worn-out rotating chair and listen to a diatribe of business talk and slander, having my attention directed to charts, PowerPoints, notes that I will later take with me in greasy printouts. He mixes market investment tips and his directives on my investments with violent banging against Asian vaginas, holes, mouths, sometimes cartoons, sometimes snuff. I am to memorize all the words he feeds me. Sometimes, he airs my own moving images and sounds, while I struggle with a choke chain in a suffocating hood – "They pay well in the Orient for this material," he chortles. I engage in abomination – "Don't you people get to eat your dogs? Well, in this country, we get the dogs to eat you." Digital feed blares my screams until they become moans and subside, then it restarts itself. "Didn't you people come up with water torture?" he asks. If I resist, or panic, he shows me documents from my home office that I'm sure I've shredded (I'm never allowed to ask how he gets them), my nightmares, the faces of the twins, photographs, edited bits and pieces of my life in a demonic montage. I rarely resist. Don't know what it is. Not the nosebleed after so much white dust up my nose, not the lullaby of screams from the TV and his seedy breath on me, maybe the humming of the monitors, something sets me to sleep. I cave in. When I wake up, he is sipping tea, strong and aromatic. Then, he orders me to leave.*

In September of 1999 — a dreadful digit followed by three lucky numbers — Emilia told Kevin point-blank that she would be leaving him, taking the twins and relocating to one of his properties of *her* choice. He looked rather amused and a touched puzzled. Having married when he was almost thirty, pushed gently by his parents and his concerned family, he had developed a jolly outlook on life along with a pudgy and arrogant build. His health was not what it used to be, he had said, internal problems, maybe an ulcer, perhaps an irritable colon. Kevin had also amassed a considerable fortune. He smiled quietly, and his eyes squinted until they were single lines. Emilia's heavy Chinese accent had abandoned her, and the clarity in her voice was unexpected and startling.

They were reading in their living room. Kevin read; Emilia sat politely, staring into the empty space before her—an evening like so many others. Kevin lifted his eyes over the newspaper and laconically suggested taking a holiday, going somewhere with the twins and his mother-in-law as soon as the kids' school was over. No expression crossed Emilia's face as she repeated the same words she'd uttered before, this time followed by a quiet sentence: "You don't seem to understand, do you?"

Kevin didn't pay any attention and told her, in a voice that was partially annoyed, partially amused, to go to bed and rest. Emilia added that she would not be going, that she had made other arrangements. Kevin noticed her, for the first time in a long time, and said "Emilia, do as I say. Go to bed." An impatient tight-lipped directive. She said no. Some minutes of normal silence fell upon the couple. The Chinese nanny with the British accent passed through the room almost imperceptibly, like an apparition, delivering one fleeting but loving look into the eyes of Emilia who was now watching Kevin intently.

Emilia said that she had found him more tolerable before, when he played hockey. (It wasn't at all in Emilia's character to sit and reminisce like this.) Kevin said that she used to show more obedience when he had some time to slap some reason into her—he said this melodiously, almost absentmindedly. Emilia said that he seemed to respond in much the same way—"You showed great obedience to your hockey playmate even after he chastised you out of jealousy for getting me pregnant"—those were indeed her exact words. They did not come out minced or broken. He called Emilia "a spiteful mail-order whore" in Chinese, and she responded in English that he had not been able to make her feel like a whore at all. "Unlike you, Kevin, I wasn't a mistress to a white man who would never look at me with pride."

*Who would have thought it possible? Not me. One more genie in a bottle, one more stray digital call. Emilia, the mail-order bride without a past, the blank-slate spouse who happens to remember dates and motives with uncanny clarity. "I remember," she said, "as clear as day the strange photographer who came to take wedding portraits, as clear as evening he returned years later to take family portraits. We'd dressed up; we'd dressed the twins in gray and dark red tweed. The photographer wore Endurables—remember?"*

*I was stunned by her sudden burst of memory, her miraculous acquisition of language, and wanted to stop her, to feel her buckle under my hand. I began to lift myself up from my favorite leather armchair, but before I could complete this motion, Emilia produced a shiny little object from her scented flowery sleeve. Not a handkerchief. She said that her name was Min Lueu and that she would like to start being called by her original name again after all these years. I could have breached the two feet between us in two easy steps and put an end to this absurd display, but before I could react Min Lueu, with a soft finger and the semblance of a smirk began to dial eight, three, nine, eight, three, nine, followed by a fatalistic number one. I could hear the numbers; I have learned to memorize the tones; I have learned much in that trailer in the suburbs. I knew the sounds associated with those numbers by heart. Deep inside of me, something ominous began to vibrate. A call.*

# MOODY BEAUTY: QUEER INCIDENT ON WESTBOUND RED-EYE

*To Svend Robinson, because all stories have three versions.*

Dear Readers: In my five years as editor of this publication I have never seen the flurry of mail that this story has brought in. It has resonated with our turn-of-the-century religion of disorders and phobias. Nothing had sparked such controversy in this otherwise peaceful neck of the woods since queers tried to build a wall in commemoration of those decimated by AIDS in the late 1990s and were met with public scorn and internal discord, or since the time we saw Sue Rodriguez's fight for her "right to die" supported by Svend Robinson, our maverick gay member of parliament.

Everybody has something to say about Mauricio Montaner, and everybody has something to say about themselves. The selection of letters reproduced in this issue is a barometer of the breadth (and breath!) of public opinion. I reluctantly admit to having met Dr. Montaner socially in the past under different circumstances. Like everyone else, I was quickly put on edge by his curious personal magnetism. Aside from this, I have little to dig out of the Pandora's box that sprang open after the flight incident, and sprang wider still after his health took such an unfortunate turn last fall. The following letters have been edited for space, and certain passages that contained the most offensive material have been left out.

*Vancouver, May 19, 1999*
Dear Editor: I don't usually write letters to the editor—I firmly object to the public nakedness of modern life, the destruction of our forests, and searing my eyes before cancer-inducing devices such as computers. However, this time I feel I have to say something about this man,

Mauricio Montaner, and what he has done. I understand the nature and suffering of Dr. Montaner's disorder. I, myself, suffer from hypoglycemia and fibromyalgia. I have had considerable grief sensitizing doctors to the nature of my problems. Over many years, I have been referred to many specialists without any of them being able to give me any satisfactory responses. Much like him, I feel like an orphan in a world where everybody seems unable to understand our malady or find a cure for it. Although I do not excuse his behaviour, I do feel the pain inflicted by the constant agony of having one's body clock out of synch. I see how he had to live at night like a desolate vampire. I am affected by sleeping disorders too and — this I write with great difficulty — a degree of hyperlibido at times. Some people here on the island truly believe I am a reclusive former American movie star. I understand why he always needed to take red-eye flights, avoid crowds, traffic, and how he might have accumulated so much anger inside. He must be a Virgo, the perfectionist, or a Gemini, like me, the curious experimenter. I have also been the object of witch-hunts for keeping odd hours and for keeping strangers away in order to stave off my multiple allergies. What happened in that overnight flight was one more unfortunate result of the corporate conspiracy to delay the circulation of air in the cabins and to cram more people in those polluting steel birds, which only serves to bring on anxiety attacks and claustrophobia, not to mention that blood clot thrombosis everyone is getting these days. One day terrible things will happen in planes: they will be used as weapons. The only positive thing that airlines have done in the last twenty years is to ban smoking — I am terribly allergic to nicotine smoke. Dr. Montaner is in my daily meditations and chants. It is truly unfortunate that he will probably never make it back from where he is now.
*Free Soulsearcher on Pender Island*

# FRANCISCO IBANEZ-CARRASCO

*Vancouver, May 20, 1999*
Dear Editor: This man is a whore, plain and simple. He's a disgrace to the gay communities in our first world societies that have worked so hard at shedding the terrible image of the predator, the infectious vector, and the oversexed individual. Almost twenty years after we registered the blip of HIV on our gaydar screens—the start of an epidemic of seismic proportions—a Canadian man, once again, bears the dubious title of being Patient Zero, now for the new millennium—the real Y2K. It is easy to see why certain older gay men are the cause of the current increase of HIV infection among vulnerable young gay men. They have found amazing treatments for AIDS, almost like a cure; they must surely have treatments for his hypoglycemia and claustrophobia, not to mention anger management training. However, nothing seems to hold back their addiction to promiscuity. They should be simply labeled "homosexuals" because sex is all they do with their "orientation." Supposedly, he was an educated man; it was his responsibility to find a solution to his medical condition. I say it loud and I say it proud that I am a healthy, clean, and safe thirtysomething gay man living with HIV. I made a mistake once. I was as young as the flight attendant in this case, and I have paid dearly for it. I would never do this again. We should all learn our lessons in life. He has given his family great grief, has squandered his opportunity to be a community role model, has robbed this young flight attendant of a bright career, and I won't even speculate about the mental health problems he must have transmitted to the young fellow. I was there once, lonely and vulnerable, and I know firsthand that queer youth need to be protected.
*Enraged in Vancouver*

*Montreál, May 20, 1999*
Dear Editor: I sign this letter with a *nom de plume* because

I work for the airline that Dr. Montaner used to fly between Vancouver and Toronto. I had the opportunity of seeing him in first class several times. Although we only had occasional exchanges, he always impressed me as a good-natured man greatly favored by nature. In case you are wondering, no, I did not get it on with him— *qu'est-ce qu'il ferait avec une sacoche comme moi?* But I doubt anyone would need to be conned into it. I can see how any young man would fall for this attractive and educated man. The photos that have been published in the media, including your publication, seem to have been taken recently and do not do justice to the man I saw several times: tall, impeccably dressed, trimmed salt-and-pepper hair, great smile, a gym-buffed body, and "other" —*j'ai ouï dire*—great attributes. I am aware that the aircraft galleys were out of food the night the incident happened on the westbound flight from Toronto. This is uncommon, and no one could have predicted the passengers would go without food for over five hours—no one, aside from his young flight attendant *beaux* who was apparently involved. As for the incident that allegedly took place earlier at the airport, we all know that airports are grand stages where flight attendants may play either sailors or *demoiselles* in distress. I must admit it is unusual to hear that someone from the tarmac crew was involved; this is a first for me. This *ménage à trois* is missing a man and nobody is saying a word about this! I'm not surprised, however, given that the tarmac crew are such macho brutes. Although we try to offer the best of ourselves in the friendly skies, there is such a thing as *en donner plus que le client en demande.* Being a young flight attendant is an *expérience formidable,* but some young men are not necessarily prepared for it.
*Doubtful Flight Attendant in Montreál*

*Scarborough, May 23, 1999*
To the Editor: I didn't even imagine there are

newspapers like this, but my good pastor from my church convinced me that it was a good idea to set the record straight so that not all people would be thinking that all Latin Americans are like this Dr. Montaner. I came to this country when I was young—not as young as this man. I understand he was a child when he came. Maybe he grew up not knowing any better and got lost on the path to God. In the last six years, my family and I follow God through our Baptist congregation in Toronto. This man grew up too North American and forgot the good ways of our good people who never adopt adultery, promiscuity, sodomy, or pederasty. I also think that men who do not do hard labor ever become fully adults and responsible—I will send my children to vocational school. I am not a prejudiced person. I am a Christian. But in my Latino culture, we all believe that some people bring bad luck and that is exactly what happened on that flight. How can anybody know who will be with us in a plane for that many hours? I think there should be a way to find out whether one is flying in decent company, much the same way they report pedophiles, terrorists, and illegal immigrants. In any case, the scene before my poor children's eyes in the middle of the night, trapped on that plane, watching these two men in the aisle was shameful. I did not intend to discover them. A deviant young woman suggested this on a television report—how low they can stoop. It was by accident. I was very drowsy, and it was dark and bumpy when I walked up to the first class lavatory. I believe in peace and social justice. I couldn't simply walk away and ignore the atrocity being committed. I didn't know where to turn to alert the passengers. Fortunately, the co-pilot and a doctor and two flight attendants came and grabbed him and made a civil arrest. My children witnessed the pornography and violence. They can't sleep at night. They feel dirty and violated. I know because I do; my wife, the entire plane does. I will initiate a civil suit. A lawyer I know is looking into that. I think this man had coming what happened to him and he belongs where he is now; we need to atone for our sins before we are in the presence of God. I am a religious and political person from Central America. (South Americans, always trying to be European, maybe accept this behaviour.) I think that the most disgusting thing a man can do is to betray one's woman and children. I think, how can this man have lied to his wife for almost ten years? My family and I pray for his children and his wife everyday.

*Central American Man in Scarborough, Ontario*

*Toronto, May 29, 1999*

I don't know what the big whoop is all about! I have heard from more raving lunatics in the last month than the ones I meet in a low-down ecstasy rave—and believe you me, you see a lot of fucked-up guys in raves! I might as well come out and say it, but don't publish my name. Yes, I knew him, and what a dude he was. Let me tell you, it ain't easy to find one more fabulous trick (and dick) than this guy. Granted, Mauricio's got his weird moments—he's a moody beauty—but nothing that wouldn't pass with a bit of ice cream or some chocolate. Other times, he would just freak out if he felt tied down or trapped. Funny thing for a dude who loved to do that to others, get my drift? But who doesn't need to eat something after banging for hours? I mean, the Duracell bunny had NOTHING on this guy. The mile-high club has become an entirely new thing since those pills that help some of these dudes stay hard through the bump and grind and turbulence over the prairies. Mauricio was a devil in disguise: when he wanted it, he wanted it bad—and what is a girl to do?

No, I didn't take a class with him, though a friend of mine did. Dry stuff, he said; not too interesting, he said; dry shit. But he introduced me to Mauricio in an after-

hours joint. He had helped this crystal queen girlfriend of mine get detoxed, get checked, and stop turning tricks. He even got him a part-time in a department store. I'm not saying he was a saint. He always made sure he got his fair share of a deal—let me tell you, that was some weird heady stuff he was into. But, unlike all the other fat greasy yard dogs out there, Mauricio was kind of classy. When I met him, we hit it off right away. He was pretty open about his being closeted to his wife and kids; so I don't know what the big deal is all about. She must have had her head in the sand all along! Who would leave a man like that, good-looking and loaded? Not me. Would you? I never saw his house, but my buddy visited Vancouver once and stayed a week in a hotel room Mauricio rented for him and saw their place and said it was fabulous. Anyway, I feel kind of sorry for the dude. He lived his life like there's no tomorrow. That's what liberation is all about. Anyway, he wasn't as untogether as the newspapers paint him out to be. And those photos! I say, leave the guy alone; he's locked away. I know a dozen crazy bitches who should be there instead. Surely the flight attendant who drove him there is still out having his share of fun, passing the creepy-crawly on—not to mention the one closeted ground crew dude that was gladly giving up his cherry beefcake and having Mauricio eat it too!
*Been There/Done That in Toronto*


*Vancouver, May 30, 1999*
Dear Editor: As an openly gay doctor in our Vancouver community, I must clarify some of the misinformation broadcast about Dr. Montaner's case over the past few weeks. I think this incident of alleged "air rage" might be best explained by the physical disorder known as "hypoglycemia," which occurs when glucose levels in the blood drop too low to fuel the body's activities and an individual becomes weak, drowsy, confused, hungry,

and dizzy. Headaches, rapid heartbeat, trembling, and irritability are also signs of low blood sugar. It might have also been caused by a combination of some licit and illicit drugs. As I reported to the police, a small bottle of amyl nitrite and a bottle of Viagra pills were found in his personal belongings. Doctors constantly see the consequences of the indiscriminate mixing of drugs. This is not to imply that my colleagues are prescribing Viagra to any gay man that requests it; it is more a case of pharmaceutical companies putting these things right under the consumer's nose.

Many of my gay patients, particularly our younger generation, firmly believe that they need to harbor little or no fear nowadays. They are out there pushing the limits of what is physically possible by ingesting a "cocktail" of recreational drugs. Survivor's guilt or envy? Who knows?

Based on the spurious coverage of the westbound red-eye incident, one can only speculate that he took a dose of Viagra while airborne and this may have adversely affected his hormonal levels of insulin and glucagons. The symptoms associated with hypoglycemia are sometimes mistaken for symptoms caused by unusual stress and anxiety, which can cause an excess production of catecholamines, resulting in symptoms similar to those of hypoglycemia. It has been reported that Dr. Montaner was a "closeted" gay man, who kept odd hours, had almost abandoned teaching for controversial academic research (allegedly on gay men's health—how ironic), and seemed to have sought exclusively the company of high-risk young men in the sex trade. I reserve any opinion on the issue of Dr. Montaner's possible "ego-dystonic" profile, which is a psychological matter not within my field of expertise.

It was through serendipitous circumstances that I found myself peripherally involved in this imbroglio. I attended to the calls of the co-pilot as he was having a hard time appeasing Dr. Montaner, and I tried to reason with him. It is accurate that one of those rapid HIV test kits available in the U.S. and showing a positive result was found on the lavatory floor. The crew asked me whether it was some form of illegal drugs, and after I responded negatively, it was flushed down.

In retrospect, this was a foolish oversight on our part. Knowing whose positive result it was would have clarified the young flight attendant's claim that he had been recently infected and that it was through this test that he found out that very night. Of course, this claim has weakened in light of what some of his relatives and acquaintances have been divulging to the media about his "other" professional activities.

Nonetheless, a clarification is still in order. We do not yet dispense "rapid HIV test kits" over the counter in Canada. They will probably be widely available in the near future, and the prospect of young men divining their fate alone and going on desperate rampages should terrify anyone who has been fighting in the AIDS trenches.

When Dr. Montaner and the young man were caught inside the first class lavatory by one of the passengers, and he was compelled to return to his seat in a state of partial undress, he also seemed emotionally unhinged. I attempted to do some triage counselling on Dr. Montaner, but he appeared too distressed to think clearly. Soon after he had to be strapped to his seat, and I returned to my seat at the back of the aircraft. The young flight attendant was kept out of sight in the back galley until after our landing.

I report these facts with no prejudice against this man. I simply need to straighten out incorrect medical information in the hope that this prevents other men like Dr. Montaner, or his young companion, from making similar mistakes. I see in our future a community in which these unfortunate incidents do not take place, where there is freedom for every gay man; this is the sincere wish of my family of choice, my life partner, and our own child.

*Dr. John P.*

*Ottawa, June 5, 1999*

Dear Editor: As In-Flight Director of this airline, it is my duty to clarify a few glaring misconceptions around the case of Dr. Mauricio Montaner on our flight 1447 from Toronto to Vancouver on January 15, 1999. It is a fact that our flight was delayed by two hours and departed at 10:30 p.m. (Eastern Standard Time) instead of the regularly scheduled time of 8:30 p.m. This was a precautionary measure taken to ensure the safety and comfort of our passengers. The allegation that some sort of squabble between two employees and a passenger had caused the holdup at Pearson International is unfounded, as is the malicious suggestion that such an incident may have been in any way related to the unfortunate food service mishap. The misplacement of the food trolleys was an extraordinary error on the part of a crew person.

In addition, it is imperative that I acknowledge all further allegations that our airline has created a monopoly in this country and that this may be negatively affecting the high quality of our services as unfair and untrue. This was not, in any way, a contributing factor toward whatever actions Dr. Montaner brought upon himself. Our personnel continue to be trained in the highest standards of hospitality service and safety.

Finally, the issues of sexual orientation and HIV status have had no bearing whatsoever on this unfortunate case — as has been intimated by the media — nor in the hiring of any of our personnel. We do not have any business in the private lives of our ground and in-flight crews and other airline representatives. The night

Dr. Montaner's medical conditions got the best of him, our on-board personnel acted diligently to try to avert his disturbing behavior. Unfortunately, and in the best interest and safety of all the flight passengers, it was absolutely necessary to disable Dr. Montaner and make a civil arrest. Our junior flight attendant is no longer with us, and this airline has laid no legal charges against him.

*Mr. Terence McPherson — In-Flight Director*

*Vancouver, June 15, 1999*

Dear Editor: Although I am not one to indulge in tittle-tattle, I see that the barrage of mail regarding the young Dr. Montaner has spun a most intricate web.

I am a lady of modest means. I live in a lovely old building in English Bay, Vancouver. It is one of the few remaining buildings amidst the collapse of all sensible architecture. I have been blessed with a generous son whose delightful wife and three children I visit often in Toronto. My son insists that I should travel comfortably, and this I do; so many years of widowhood can make one very lonely. I often prefer to return to Vancouver late at night. A good friend of mine comes and fetches me at the airport—such a maze of aluminum, glass, and unattractive native artifacts that is; it is easy for a woman of my years to get lost there.

Travelling on my own often allows me to meet all kinds of surprising characters. Such was the case when I made Dr. Mauricio Montaner's acquaintance on two separate occasions. The first one must have been a year ago. I was impressed by how extremely handsome, smart, and well-spoken Dr. Montaner was. My late husband, Alfred, never gave enough credit to people with accents, and I have never agreed that this, or the color of their skin, is important.

When I travel, I most often occupy a seat in the very back row of business class, next to the lavatories, and tend to strike up a conversation with my fellow passenger. The second time I saw Dr. Montaner, I clearly remembered him from our first encounter; although he seemed almost agitated by the time he sat down next to me—flying upsets some claustrophobic people a great deal. He was almost the last one to board the plane, and we had been sitting at the gate for quite some time then.

At last, we seemed ready to leave. The purser explained that one of the reasons for the delay was the necessity to comply with airline regulations that there should be one crew member for every forty passengers. A young flight attendant had been brought on board at the last minute.

Dr. Montaner and I had a lovely conversation for most of the departure from L. B. Pearson Airport. It was about what a fine prime minister he had been and how appropriate it was that an important airline hub had been named in his honour. I was impressed with Mauricio's knowledge of Canadian history after he told me he had not been born in Canada. While we talked, the young flight attendant gave us the safety instructions. I think the video system was out of order. I thought it would be a long trip without one of those bad movies. The instructions were amusing—the young man was very nervous and cute—even though no instructions are as useful as a good deal of prayer when flying through the turbulence over Manitoba or Saskatchewan.

Soon after taking off, I settled into that queer and comforting drowsiness induced by the humming of the engines. It reminds me of my dear Alfred energetically using our Hoover in the midmorning. Frankly, that was a rather tedious habit. I would have preferred him to do other things, but Alfred retired early and adopted a few peculiar habits. This is why I understand some of the otherwise apparently strange customs observed by Dr. Montaner, whose age, I might add, is around my husband's age at the time he passed away.

We must have been airborne for about forty-five minutes when I woke up from my brief respite and I could hear the clacking of safety belt buckles like castanets, people wowing and chattering about a mistake that had just been announced over the loudspeakers — who can hear those announcements over the tremendous roar of the engine? In any case, I found out from Dr. Montaner that no food or beverages had been brought onboard and that we should "fasten our seat belts" and expect a "bumpy ride" — my dear Alfred always used that phrase when he saw trouble on the horizon. He had lifted those remarks from *All About Eve*, his favourite movie of all times. None of this news bothered me in the least; at my age, late dinners do not sit properly, much less during such long periods of inactivity. However, it had evidently created some tension among the staff. I could see the eyes of the other flight attendants throwing daggers at their newly arrived colleague. It was as if they were blaming him for that food fiasco. I felt sorry for the young but rather frazzled and scrawny man. In turn, when he came out of the cubicle — I think it is called "the galley" — his flushed eyes glared our way, and I thought that was odd because it made me feel that we had something to do with this mishap.

The turbulence became frightful, and the captain had turned off the cabin lights so everybody had to quiet down eventually — quite a racket they had going, like spoiled children; they wanted to be fed! This is a young generation that has not gone through two world wars, and hand-to-mouth, and make-do. I know what it was like; I was young but I remember; and I am grateful for it. I don't need to eat every hour on the hour simply because I am soaring God's skies in an aluminum rocket. Good grief, I don't even need to go to the bathroom that often! But, Dr. Montaner did go to the bathroom an unusual number of times.

It was dark in the first class cabin. No one was reading or watching movies, but I always keep an eye about myself when I am in public spaces — one never knows. I am not blind; there are certain things young people do. My children sometimes misbehaved when we travelled; so did Alfred who preferred trains so we often took the Canadian across the prairies, and stayed at the fabulous Chateau Lake Louise. He was as restless as our children sometimes, but nothing that a sip of scotch wouldn't remedy. Certainly Alfred would not have resorted to any kind of medication — these days everybody seems to take tablets to prompt every single emotion as if they were switches in a telephone console. I am no psychiatrist, but I can see that so many pills can make one very eccentric.

I don't know from where our scrawny flight attendant produced some water, but I saw the big diamond blue pill that Dr. Montaner ingested and the terrible effect it had on him. In half an hour he had become very fidgety and finally got up to go to the washroom. By the time he came back, he was calm and had a strange aroma about him. It smelled like the liquid Alfred used to clean his collection of acetate records. Some people have the strangest chemical reactions to medicines. But Dr. Montaner got restless again, and the young flight attendant came and tried to calm him down by whispering in his ear. Later, he accompanied him to the lavatory once more. I thought poor Dr. Montaner would be indisposed — the ride was certainly very bumpy that night.

I believe that the so-called "air rage" incident occurred when a short brown man with an accent tried to make his way into the small first class bathroom and found them there. I can barely turn my neck without causing a crick, but I could see that the young flight attendant was busy helping Dr. Montaner and could not assist the short man with an accent, the one sitting with the children at the head of the coach section. Although the young flight attendant politely gestured to him that he should use the lavatories at the rear of the plane, he refused to do this. I saw him go back to his seat and come back to try to pry the door open a couple of times. After the second or third try, the short man with an accent began to complain louder and louder. The rest of the unfortunate incident has been repeated many times. Dr. Montaner got so agitated, the poor man, and soon after he had to be restrained. Once covered with a blanket, he began to ask for sugar or food.

Unfortunately, his requests could not be met, and he gradually became more ill and spouted fairly incoherent and scandalous things. This seemed a compelling reason for the co-pilot to come and slap him terribly hard, and for that other man to administer God knows what medication that left Dr. Montaner with his head hanging to one side and babbling. This is very much the way my Alfred looked the day he had his stroke. The cabin crew offered me a seat at the rear of the plane or one of those small crew seats in front if I wanted, but I had no fear, only a great deal of pity that this unfortunate incident had happened. I did not talk to Dr. Montaner anymore, but I could hear his muffled sobs under the blanket; it was frightful; and I saw a drop or two of blood on the tip of his left index finger. Later, they turned the lights off, but the crew kept a close check on us.

Sometimes it is better to sweep everything under the rug. Alfred always said, "Those who live in glass houses..." or so the saying goes. It's so true, and our house had plenty of glass. Alfred did so much work on it, even the curtains. Such taste he had; he could even sew! My heart goes out to the poor man whom I last saw babbling, tied to his seat in first class, and covered with an airline throw.

*Mrs. Adelaide McNaughton*

# MOODY BEAUTY: QUEER INCIDENT ON WESTBOUND RED-EYE

*Halifax, July 2, 1999*

I have known Dr. Montaner for quite some time, and he does not deserve what is in store for him. To protect his family, he kept a polite silence about what can be considered the less-inspiring aspects of his life—isn't this an essential Canadian custom? I know he has devoted his life to the care of his wife and children, and to his career. I also know that secretly he might have cursed the Latino roots that compelled him to get married when he was too young, barely eighteen years old, to better fit into the stifling mold for British Columbia's academics. He played the grateful political-refugee-poster-boy for as many years as his wife played the uptown-girl-turned-political-activist after a single Canada World Youth exchange in Guatemala.

It is understandable that in the last years Dr. Montaner would make complicated academic arrangements to stay away from his overbearing family for long periods. Dr. Montaner has struggled for years to be recognized in his field, the humanities, a field that for all its politically correct "song and dance" is oppressive. We are a bunch of sourpusses on the bottom rung of the Canadian university system and intensely self-conscious about it. It is no wonder that Dr. Montaner would start to show signs of erosion after so many years of attempting to escape his relegation to the rank of "assistant professor." Having had the chance to work for Dr. Montaner as a research assistant, I know that he respected his students very much, and that he greatly contributed to stemming mediocrity in that small university department. His current research on young male sex-trade workers and sexual health might have had something to do with his past—it is not uncommon to see academics exorcise their demons in their professional work—but I believe his research was also genuinely motivated by a sense of social justice.

I witnessed Dr. Montaner's gradual withdrawal

from undergraduate teaching and transformation into a nocturnal person. On the West Coast, he mostly kept his Toronto hours, always living three hours ahead. This allowed him to be up late into the night and meet those who would eventually become his research subjects. This has always been criticized as unethical, although I know few scientists who have *not*, in one way or another, used the skills of personal seduction and charisma in the pursuit of their plans.

Dr. Montaner was one cool cat, swift of mind and mood, a man who listened to Steely Dan, Ron Sexmith, and Shuggie Otis, and who appreciated a chilled martini, an Armani suit over his firm shoulders, and the vigorous company of blue-collar young men — many Marxist academic busybodies would not forgive his refusal to keep on suffering on the cross as a political refugee forever reclaiming his Latino roots. (I have seen one too many professors' lives turn into a shrine for one cause or another.)

Dr. Montaner had anything but abandoned his family. He had done more than his fair share for them. His daughters were adults; his wife always seemed quite content to maintain a busy social schedule; and financial problems were not a primary concern. I know he had carefully provided for the college fund of his daughters. If anything, they are indulged creatures and not the victims of an unloving and absent father as the media has portrayed. I think we often see things as we want to see them, or deny them when it is convenient for us.

It will be hard for everyone to understand Dr. Montaner's reality, much more now that he has been virtually declared insane and abandoned by his family. What loneliness must he feel. Even those of us who have caught a mere glimpse of his intricate and fascinating personality have now been placed in the profoundly uprooting and anti-intellectual "witness protection program" we call academic relocation. The "closet" envelopes a desolate and barren landscape, but no one is alone in there. Whoever theorized that homosexuals have a secure corner in that landscape ignores that we all have a separate and barren piece of land in our hearts, some sort of black hole that drains our dark secrets, our hopes, and dreams.

*Disillusioned PhD Student in Halifax*

Thus, dear readers, ends this tale of uncertain ending. The characters are still out there — all of them that is but Dr. Montaner, whose mental health — we are told by medics — has deteriorated severely and whose future looks grim without the support of his family, colleagues, community, and with the prospect of developing AIDS at such a late age. His family declined all our requests for interviews, and so did the local police who seem to be halfheartedly investigating the case.

The moral of this story? There is no moral when there are so many claims; there is only uncertainty and anxiety left behind. This case will probably recede into the darker corners of our memories as a curious and isolated incident, but I wonder whether or not it embodies a new harvest of *petit scandale* to divert our attention away from the complexity of human nature and toward a theater of shadows not unlike reality TV shows.

# ADAM'S INDEX

*"Did you ever go clear?"*
— Leonard Cohen

Only the twins could have connected the dots that took Adam from Penticton to Vancouver to Toronto and back to Vancouver where he made his three final stops at Richards' Service Club, the house on Woodland Drive, and Stanley Park. People and their stories get lost easily in the little bitch city that is Vancouver, particularly when going through the revolving doors of the neighborhood that is called the West End. This lackadaisical fingertip of land sometimes seems quite disengaged from the rest of the city. In the 1980s and 1990s, Vancouver's West End lost many of its inhabitants to the plague, and the vacancy left by souls and bodies gave way to migrating families who coveted the perceived safety and charm of its dutiful homos who — who would have thought? — turned out to be hypermasculine, didn't fuck children, and had the clean "lifestyle" of well-trained pets. The West End lives up to its postcard-perfect image and refuses to pay heed to the murdered prostitutes, to the drug derelicts, or to the memory of old or killed gay men. On weekend nights, there is an eerie feeling of a land haunted by young bored men coming from the suburbs to clobber their homoerotic fantasies made flesh: the hookers, unsuspecting passersby at night, and fags. Nowhere else is Vancouver's old seaport harshness and ambivalence more plain than in Stanley Park, the pride of Vancouver, the jewel in the crown of the whore. It behaves as an insufferably goody-two-shoes family resort by day — its unsanitary century-old beaches strewn with logs and gray sands that are infested with the stench of hot dogs and cheap sunscreen lotion in the summer, invaded by rats, screeching children, old folks, and giddy Asians and Americans tourists on rollerblades wobbling along with their digital cameras, cells, and dreadful polyester getups. By night, Stanley Park doubles as a pent-up little cauldron of sordid but illustrative northern gothic stories.

The park caps the corner tip of Denman and Davie, home to what little gay commerce there is in the city. Off to the southeast side, and closer to the downtown business district that empties out each night, the worn-out Dufferin Hotel looms over the nightlife as if it were a crooked hairpiece. This establishment takes in a motley crew of characters. There is a sprinkle of Latinos, Native transvestites, alcoholics, and damaged smooth operators. And there are homeless young men who grind their behinds on a little makeshift stage at the back bar, trying hard to follow the syncopated rhythms from the defective sound system. After two sets and some languid applause, a few five-dollar tips, and a few more watered down high-balls at the bar proffered by badly bleached blonds, sex tourists, and despondent old men, they go and tweak in the back lot—"get that thing goin', cutie pie, will ya! I'll be with'cha in a minute."

It was at The Dufferin where Adam arrived from Penticton and started his city life fresh as a snowball. He dove into that hectic scene and befriended the other boys shipwrecked on the glammed-up urban core. Adam learned about the trade from the stories peppered with joint puffs and laughter like shrieks of nocturnal seagulls. Someone had lifted Marc's date, a balding old boyfriend, from the table where they were sitting when he'd gone to the bathroom to snort some crystal. Last week, someone had followed Trinity all the way to The Regal and caused a scandal by screaming, "You are not a girl, motherfuckin' cunt. Gimme my man back, or I'll cut ya good." Trinity showed up next day with a bloody lower lip and a shiner and confided in the manager that she had sent the disgruntled lover to the ER—"The sonofabitch wanted to get me. I *had* to do it. It's the *cahones* kicking in from time to time, darling."

No one recounted a story as grandly as Trinity. Trinity and Adam never laid hands on each other, that way. "We're two-spirit sisters," she said immediately after he tried one time. Trinity helped cement Adam's reputation. She was the only other person beside the twins who could have pieced together what may have happened.

And as for the house on Woodland Drive, it still opens its weary eyes every morning and sighs and yawns; it is kept alive. It dons more makeup on its face now, like an old prostitute. But it still harbors love at its very heart. The morning that Adam went clear, the house accumulated a tear or two in its tired gutters.

Adam's index finger was his compass: to guide him through the architecture of bodies and to assert his direction in the happenstance of every day. The day he lost the top segment of it, he lost his sense of direction. With one sharp swat, destiny clawed back a great deal of Adam's confidence as well. Testosterone and adrenaline surged through the body he had laboriously shaped into a sculpture as defiant as a forefather statue in a public square that day, and then out of him like a barely contained shudder. *Whoosh.*

For the day Adam lost the tip of his finger, his hand modeling career was over, a fleeting course along a path that had even taken him before the cameras as an uncredited extra in the first season of *Queer As Folk*—this being his major claim to fame and a salient item in his bartending résumé.

Nightclubbing in Toronto's Church and Wellesley area, the ghetto, away from his native land, soon wore thin. He swallowed dry and with much chagrin he reviewed all he had done to escape his parochial middle-class life in Penticton: his sojourn in Vancouver with its pompadoured Italian real estate agents in cheesy motels; the white brokers in gray suits; the bingo nights at the Legion Hall with drunken longshoremen; the yellowish spit of Asian slumlords; his listless dancing at The Dufferin, and Richards' Service Club. Adding it all up he had managed to keep his thick nine inches intact, but some of his serene bravado had flown like spirits into the night. He felt again like one lonely Indian in a big city, and his next destination, the Big Apple, seemed a world away. From that moment on, when Adam was mad, or in a nasty drunk, he would brandish his stump in the air to point at ghosts. He would lean the stump against the foreheads, chests, necks, and cavities of his lovers, and it was as if he had punctured their skin—it unnerved them so.

Having half an index finger would no longer allow him to boldly survey new territories, he thought. It became clear that there was not a hope in hell for him to model for Martika Sveena's new audiovisual installation project, the soon-to-be-shot reenactment of the Sistine Chapel fresco in which Neelambar, an upcoming Indo-Canadian porn star, blue as Vishnu, touches the tip of Adam's index finger with the index finger of one of his four hands. This was to be followed by another tableaux satirizing E.T. touching a young Drew Barrymore, and one more of Adam's index finger touching God's enigmatic and portentous erection—the index finger without a nail. The project was being touted as an "ironic/iconic pronouncement against postcolonialism by subverting and recontextualizing a classical image in order to recover the spirit stripped away from original peoples."

Adam now fell about two inches short, and Martika rolled over in her bed with a feigned headache, went to sleep, and eventually lost Adam's cell number, thus putting an absentminded end to her neurotic casting-couch calls and to Adam's transition from shopping catalogs to video art, Warhol-style, three decades too late. When he saw his hopes billowing away like evaporating steam in the cold crisp Toronto morning, he went back to his part-time starring roles in the cheap digital-camera porn movies for sale on the Internet.

No one seemed to recognize the twentysomething young man from the well-known hand modeling shots — a friend in the skies handling Air Canada duty free catalog items — or from the video installations in Parkdale's own Rehab Video Festival of "blue rare footage." That aloof clique of artistes dropped him from their attention, a fate worse than being gimp. And no longer did a notorious video maker — considered by some to be emerging as Canada's own Derek Jarman — chase after him with a predatory appetite for inspiration and respiration. Nor did he keep his promise to introduce Adam to Bruce LaBruce or Attila Lukacs when they were in town. And a punk Nova Scotian fiddler that had shocked audiences two years earlier by having Adam piss on him in a bathroom stall as part of the "Liquid Reality" installation suddenly ran dry. And a noted anthropology professor he had met at Sneakers had lost his interest in him too. Instead, the professor had married a breathing and walking Cowichan wife, a perfect item to add to his impressive collection of West Coast native artifacts. At twenty-eight, Adam's dreams of fame and fortune had been cut down to a size smaller than Toronto's dream of being a world-class city that never sleeps.

The day he lost his finger: Adam's blood is surging to his head, to the raw nerve endings of his cockhead, to the roots of his long jet black hair, his internal wiring overloading with pulsations, adrenaline, and a craving to trample on everything like a bucking horse. He begins to feel a rage electrify his limbs and the skipping of his heart. *Can't be the ecstasy pill*, he thinks. He has tried it many times before. He never loses control. *Can't be this weird place made to look like an abandoned motel*, he considers. They are shoving and pushing—it is partly pent-up heat and partly loathing. A single bulb in the raunchy bathroom gets knocked out. Some bluish fluorescent light from outside tints both of their bodies. No words are mixed into the rarefied air. The air is blue. Adam is doused in fury and hunger—they both are. Adam has done this before, coldly, like a child dissecting a live insect with a mix of awe and repulsion, wing by wing, antler by antler. He used to do it unbeknownst to his foster parents, muffled by the shadows of the night. His mood today flares up more potent than before. The rusty tap water trickles like a metronome and collects with the urine on the tile floor. Adam bends him over and pushes his face into the puddle while he bites hard on his warm and supple darkness.

The alley behind the bathroom has garbage strewn all over it. It is desolate except for a few rats that meander about carrying on their grisly chores. Feverishly, Adam's hand guides his stark erection and he drills into the man dry and coarse, grunting, "Yeah fuckin' let me in, ya mutherfuker." The man, bigger in muscles and in silence, complies as he is fiercely taken from behind, his grimace signaling pain through every pore, and there is a quick splintering of his eyesight into pixels. His breathing is arrested as one of Adam's hands goes over his head, pulls his hair, and then tightens around his sturdy trachea. "Who's my bitch now, eh?" Adam probes. "Who's my bitch?" The ghost memory of Father O'Malley, the dormitory inspector, looming over him in the complicit darkness intoxicates him with an otherworldly brew of rage and craving. His clothes are soiled; his muscles are hardened under a torn shirt. Two shadows brawl behind the translucent bathroom doors of the dormitory gymnasium, their ghostly shadows projected by the full moon of middle night, and again today, two shadows snatch pieces of clothing and struggle.

At the end of the narrow dark corridor there is a door where the sign "reception" can be read in crimson 1960s lettering barely illuminated by a single naked bulb within. A decrepit desk lamp sits next to a heavy black telephone that never worked—movie-set props never *really* work. From this office, the thudding of Adam's pelvis against the man's ass is barely audible. One of the man's ribs cracks; a ligament is ripped like a canvas sail laughing savagely in a storm. With both hands, Adam stretches the man's ass, reaching deeper—he is dogging the way he has been dogged many times before. He is cool, almost distant. He ploughs the way he ploughed into Richards' Service Club and out of the whore city. Raw, reddened, and dizzied by the throttling and shoving, the man's face smashes against a wall of cold tiles. The grimy shower door shatters, and Adam exhales a single deep groan.

Panting, Adam notices a viscous fluid covering everything. He brutally pulls out of his filled bitch—there is no escaping DNA. The strong man holds his head, wheezing, almost whimpering as he wipes a streak of blood and sweat from his forehead. He tries to clean Adam's face dry with his blistered tongue. He tries to kiss Adam; a peace offering that Adam rejects—"Get away from me, ya groveling bitch." Adam pushes him away. The man picks himself up as if lifting a burden and slowly stumbles step after step out of the movie set. Adam pulls himself together quickly. He is not done with him yet. He intends to follow his willing prey and assault him once more over the dusty reception desk, in plain view of the glassy eyes of the stuffed birds. Instinctively, Adam begins to count his own fingers, one by one, not wanting to bleed anymore. In the distance, a motorbike clears its hoarse throat and speeds away. When he gets to count the tip of his index finger, Adam realizes it is missing!

By the time Adam arrived at the Vancouver airport he didn't recognize the strange totems topped by heads with bulging-eyed heads and scraggly hair. The town had put on makeup to the point of being unrecognizable. To grow, she pays the price that small town girls most often pay in seaports, especially when wanting to embark on swankier seas; she had become a whore. She had put on those high-heeled architectural stilettos that had never been properly broken in and sprayed herself with whiffs of grand airs.

Vancouver walks funny but looks perky, a nice piece of ass, a pearl of the Pacific Northwest. A damsel in a little distress, she exhales a little Marilyn Monroe sigh, and continues to cry rain forest tears as the red necks of the woods, the blue collar mavericks in drunken pubs, sleazy politicians, public servants, and grubby activists fuck her good and then leave her reeking of dreariness like yesterday's news. Here's some cash. "Pack your tits into an uplifting bra, honey, and go hit Robson Street and Yaletown. Get a load of Hollywood North. Get yourself something pretty." Not in vain, someone has called her Lotus Land, a fitting name for a glacial geisha.

Three stops. Adam, upon his return to Vancouver, and before going clear, made three stops. The first was in the morning at Richards' Service Club. He called the old manager the day before. Adam's voice, having lost its juvenile twinkle, startled the old fag. He coughed and spat, but he soon regained his poise. He asked Adam point-blank whether he wanted to see *any* of Richard's relatives and "what the fuck are you *after* tracking him down like this and calling his number?" Adam said no, no to everything, calmly. He said he only wanted to see the place one more time. There was a prolonged silence at the other end of the line. The old manager told Adam that he would be loading up a few leftovers from the place the next day, that he himself would be as good as gone by Friday.

Adam ventured a general question about how Richard's family was doing. In abrupt grunts, the old fag said that as soon as Richard had croaked of AIDS, they, the family, had put the old building up for sale—"not a moment too soon...motherfuckers." One of the twins, the one in the movies, had packed himself into leather chaps and jacket, shiny clasps, belt, and helmet, and had gone roaming Montana, Wyoming, and Minnesota with other angels on a beautiful cream-and-crimson-red Indian Spirit. "Betcha you would've wanted to go on *that* ride, eh?" interrupted Adam. "Fuck you," snapped the old fag at the other end of the line. "You an' yer bad ass. Thanks to you, they didn't even talk to each other at their father's memorial." He finished his cursory explanation by saying that the second twin was in town, doing the usual, stitching up corpses, cutting and stitching, happily married, a proud parent, happy to have buried his deviant father...and he said that their mother might be dying soon, hopefully. "You saw her, didn't you? Crotchety old bitter hag she is."

Next morning, when Adam showed up at the condemned building, he found the manager hauling out a few dilapidated bathroom fixtures and some black plastic bags. It took some convincing to get the sullen fag to let him wander around the second floor for a while. Once Adam reached upstairs and tentatively stepped inside, it was like he was alone on a film soundstage, like he was hearing the silence crawl up the bare walls of an abandoned residential school—an immense hollowness that makes time stop ticking—and the lull in Adam's heart was followed by a murder of ghosts, a flock of slightly audible voices that fluttered in. The abrasive caresses of worn-out white towels rustled against the grainy walls. Adam could hear the shedding of dry skin, the smell of foul and sweet underarms, of inner thighs, lean and fat, and crotches—all tightly fastened by straps and belts around buttocks, calves, napes, and palms. Five generations of phantoms came out smiling lecherously as Adam put his ear to the ground and listened to the panting of conquests and defeats. Almost ten years ago, one night before he had been "discovered," before making his midnight round of the Boystown stroll around the corner on Davie and Homer, turning tricks to get some cash going, Adam had come in. To keep the high crystal clear, Adam dropped by Richards' Service Club. Richard happened to be there, in the back office, quarreling with one of his teenage sons.

Lights were dimmed, and the patrons could scarcely see the shadowy outlines of their profiles or the path between the two severe rows of cubicles equipped with prison benches, ragged sheets, and limp pillows. In the winter, the attendants had to strategically perch buckets over precarious planks that crisscrossed the top of the cubicles to collect leaking rain. Dressed in skimpy outfits to endure the heat, they went about their miserable hostessing with absent expressions, rarely peeking at the contorted bodies, just kicking aside limbs strewn into the narrow corridors so they could enter a vacant cubicle to get it ready for the next customer. "Number 19, there is a room available for you. Come immediately to the front door with your locker room belongings and key." These meat market announcements over the loudspeakers would interrupt Rock 99.5 QZFM and its incessant siphoning of songs by Heart, Loverboy, Glass Tiger, and Billy Idol into the frantic darkness. And the band played on.

Adam recalled that when it used to get busy in there it was like standing really close to a pretty girl in the

Roncesvalles streetcar during rush hour, getting a hard-on, and pinning her against the railing like a helpless butterfly—that is how Adam had met Martika. He also recalled that first night he had seen one of Richard's sons stomping down the Club stairs, deep-track biker boots stepping down confidently, one step at a time, helmet in hand. They had exchanged one guarded glance.

Although statistically almost half of the population of Greater Vancouver is not of Anglo descent, only a sprinkle of Asians, East Indians, Iranians, and Latinos populate the hard-core scene in Vancouver. They come in different shapes and sizes, bearing different states of mind. Often, they follow closely the roles available to them, acting timidly and lurking, not swaggering aggressively like the Anglos. Often, the city slowly disrobes them of self-assuredness with her long spinsterlike fingers, with her sweet reproach, as if browbeating disobedient residential school children into civilized submission. In fact, she is priming them to fuck them up. By the time they make their way into the tubs, they have adopted the politesse of dutiful Canadian immigrants. They often take their share of time to peek wide-eyed over the broad shoulders of others as they sneak their way into the network of glory holes at Richards' Service Club.

When Adam came into the Vancouverite scene, he was a young and rare outsider. Not many Indians are seen in bars or bathhouses, and Adam carried an unconventionally intense presence. His dark features held the muted nobility of an exotic human specimen whose savage soul has been captured in a sepia daguerreotype. His shyness came across as aplomb, and his poverty as the desirable "shabby chic" look peddled by glossy magazines, all of this without his ever having forced himself onto a diet or a treadmill.

Richard met Adam standing at the far end wall of the Dufferin Bar, his hands buried in his pockets, leaning against the wall, looking ahead, not looking at him—Yes, they had met before. "You were behind the counter at that bathhouse," Adam muttered. "No, I don't want a beer." No, he would not strip for fucking twenty bucks, he added later. Yeah, he could use some getting high right then, not there though. Once inside old Richard's truck, Adam asked him point-blank whether he had "a boy." No. Adam pressed the point—"Who was that guy, you know, he looked my age, leaving the tubs, the one who was yelling at you the other night?" Richard did not respond and began to crush some rock with a gold VISA. He didn't stop grinding when Adam announced that he was "in need of a place to crash." Later that night, Adam did the grinding on Richard's wrinkled old buttocks to get some cash for a place to stay. The old man's haggard face flat against the driver's side windowpane of his polished four-wheel-drive truck. His crystal dick and balls dangling like weird Christmas ornaments.

In the months ahead much of the same trade was to come Adam's way, garnering him enough to find a room to rent, away from the downtown core, enough to party and play. Like any nineteen-year-old would, Adam had dreamed that there would be a great deal of emotion involved, that the sad songs would come true, slowly dripping their syrup into the scratches and grooves of lovemaking, that this would be his first romance, his endless love. He imagined himself in the last scene of *An Officer and a Gentleman*, carried away in a muscular pair of starched white uniformed arms to a place up there, where they belong. That would be only the beginning of his movie. The first flick, it didn't have to last long, but it would happen—magazines and TV had told him so.

Of all the "street family" Adam became acquainted with

in downtown Vancouver, Trinity was the best at causing
mischief. She was plainspoken, brutal, and a good pal.
When "work" at Richards' Service Club and other things
in Adam's life had run their course, Trinity was there to
put it all in perspective. She could have been in her late
twenties—who actually knew? She had a glorious body.
It was the color of Douglas fir bark and, having never
been snipped, she possessed the indomitable heart of a
two-spirit girl. And boy was she ever ugly! Her Adam's
apple vibrated deeply, and her teeth danced all over the
place. But she managed to turn any serious curse into a
favor of nature. That night Trinity smuggled herself into
Richards' Service Club at about 2:00 a.m. by tucking her
long jet black hair inside a touque, erasing the soft
makeup from her eyelashes and lips, and wearing jeans
and a rain jacket. Once she was inside and had managed
to get a cubicle, a major feat at that time of the early
morning, she metamorphosed back into her real self.

Richards' Service Club was for nearly three decades
a bastion of unrepentant, unsentimental men fucking
each other, where possession of a thick skin, a pliable
hole, a deep throat, or a firm boner were nine-tenths of
the law that regulated the fluctuating market of misery
and might. The old gay sauna was frequented by trolls,
drunks, rough trade, middle-aged men in worn-out
leather costumes, frayed cutoffs, tight T-shirts, and other
garments that would seem ridiculous in the light of day.
In the damp twilight of Richards' Service Club, they
accrued a patina of unbridled desire. These were men
with hard-earned habits, acquired tastes, and capable of
uncanny bodily feats. By 2:15 a.m., Trinity opened her
door and her legs to the eager passersby. At that time of
the night, the crowd was engorged with the young and
crazed, redolent from new leather outfits and deodorant,
the sybarites who had danced themselves into a frenzy,
all the while untouchable, chastely kissing their
boyfriends goodnight after the last call, and who now

would turn around to receive them, faceless, at the tubs. Stomping around like bitches in heat, sniffing, bottom-feeding, demanding with an utter sense of entitlement some compensation for almost three decades of sex-, alcohol-, and drug-prohibition, hollering to be bucked roughly by as many as possible. They saw in Trinity a kindred beast, unleashed, and they flocked in. When Adam peeked through the ivy of limbs, he saw Trinity totemic and fierce, with a Rottweiler crawling up her back. Even bitches would turn into riders in Trinity's presence. Adam saw the teeth of others clenching her breasts. One adoring gargoyle-like old man was kneeling before her, devouring her genitals. Others would extend their fingers and try to lay a hand on this deity — Our Lady of the Cubicles. Adam looked at the dog on her back, and for mere seconds he caught a glimpse of an Indian chief tattoo on a tense bicep. The tattooed man's squinting little blue eyes caught sight of Adam's and swiftly turned away as he kept gnawing and shoving at Trinity's back.

When the sauna attendants got wind of what was going on and became irate and told her she had to leave, Trinity did not back down. The leathery Rottweiler mounted on her back did not stop shoving as she began to scream — "Ya motherfuckers! Ya go crazy for pussy...and you call yourself fags." Her queer rage only fueled the thirst of the bodies attached to her — "You fucking trick babies. Drink. Ride. Give yer Indian bitch som'thing back, ya motherfuckers." It took a good half hour for the attendants to swat away all the ravenous dogs from around her, to get her to dress up, and walk her out, pushing her all the way. Adam, who had stepped to her defense, was also unceremoniously shown the door.

"We got ran out of town, Shirley," Trinity joked once they hit the pavement. "Ain't it the Indians' lot in life, eh?" She pulled herself together in two shakes of her tail.

"Fuck it. Let's go to Toronto," she invited. Adam hesitated. "What? Can't you? Yeah, 'cause you got something going on. With the owner? Fucking troll. He'll drop your sorry ass as soon as he's done with ya, Shirley," Adam still hesitated. "So? What stops you, Shirley?" Adam did not say a word. "I'd say you're in love...with him? Or someone else? These whiteys are trouble. C'mon, let's go to fucking Toronto, Shirley!" And so they did.

That very same early morning, Adam went to the old gabled and shingled house in the East Side, on Woodland Drive, to pick up his clothes. If he had woken up Melanie, she did not come out of her room. Maybe she was already awake. Often, Kevin had to get up very early to go work in the hospital where he was doing his residency. Indeed, Adam noticed that Kevin's duffel bag was not sitting next to the front door. He collected his stuff and did not lock the front door on his way out. He did not look back. In the chilly morning light he headed toward the Greyhound station.

Adam made three stops before he went clear. His second stop was at the house on Woodland Drive. Melanie was there; she seemed absentminded, not surprised. There wasn't much said between the two of them. There was no sign of a sweet-tempered little girl playing around the house. Adam did not ask where Jane had gone because he'd come here for other intentions, not to reclaim fatherhood, if there was any fatherhood to be reclaimed. Melanie let him in by simply stepping aside. While he walked around tentatively, she went and sat down in the luminous kitchen that was now decked in 1940s reconditioned chrome appliances and dozens of labeled canisters carefully aligned on shelves. Adam walked about, and Melanie allowed him. Melanie leaned over the coral Formica table and lowered her head over her crossed arms. Her eyes remained fixed on a list of chores carefully written out: a house project she had to complete for her Thursday-evening interior decorating class; her Friday Hatha Yoga session; and a grocery list headed by the purchase of more energizing soy drinks. It all needed to be done before Kevin came home — that was often late — and much later after Jane was dropped off by the school bus.

Melanie matched the decor as if she had been Feng Shui-ed in with the rest of the household objects. Six years ago, the day Adam arrived on Woodland Drive looking for a room, she too was there, the same Melanie, but so different. Then, she barely dressed in flowery paper-thin dresses and an aroma of eighteen springs swirled about her and her cascade of blonde curls. Melanie had added a constant flux to the house by installing smiles in each of its corners. She didn't really know many things, and her initial interest for Adam came from the textbooks on Women Studies and Native Studies she had read in her first general year in the Liberal Arts program at Simon Fraser University. Sitting on the spacious front porch, she had devoured these books.

The house on Woodland Drive used to be different then. A dilapidated 1900s Vancouver Box that had been a neglected rental for years. Its droopy two eyes above the porch — two long guillotine windows — had watched the trails of heavy cotton dresses as they dragged though the mud, the unemployed sawmill workers and coal miners as they roamed the area looking for menial work, the mechanical insect that was the first street car as it crawled insecurely up the gravel road, and the impoverished Indians as they were run out of town and up the hill toward Coquitlam. Although the 1970s were extremely cruel to it — its walls had been bastardized with wooden siding, the ceiling with acoustic tiles, and the fir floors had been slapped with sheets of cheap linoleum — the house clung to its small remaining detailing with that trembling despair with which old folks clasp packages, lockets, and forlorn love letters. The decorative brackets, the hot-air furnace, the cast-iron vents, and the narrow but incongruously majestic set of treads and risers, sided by a wooden balustrade, whimsical spindles, and topped by pillars and carved round newels on both ends, all that had been spared the sleazy hand job of modernity.

Life at the house was always young and fleeting when Adam first arrived. Weekly, one of its many and transient occupants would come up with a new political or spiritual cause. It was hard for anyone to try to keep up, but Adam navigated through these vogues and rituals calmly. He was often excused by virtue of his dark skin and slightly slurred Native accent.

The refurbished rooms where Adam stood at present had little or nothing left of the run-down, haphazardly painted, patched-up house where he had once lived. Adam had walked in to see a flawlessly tummy-tucked and face-lifted old maiden, and yet, he could sense the coiling and looping of the many motions once executed in the air. Today, he didn't hear echoes of dialogue or see translucent apparitions. But he divined movements, the everyday motions recorded in the air between the walls, in the staircase, in the attic rooms, across the long hall, or buried in the basement. He divined the restlessness of young lovemaking that had gone stale; a curse that the presence of Jane, Melanie's child, had not been able to exorcise.

Melanie's myriad giddy gestures — putting on a thin Chinese satin robe after sex, running modestly to the only bathroom on the second floor, trying not to get caught by the other roommates — could charm anyone who came in close contact. Soon after Adam moved in — from the streets where he had been hanging out, couch-surfing — the third and fourth roommates left the household. And then, there were three, at least for a while. Having no other female roommate to usurp her reign of loveliness over the house, Melanie became the matrix of all things sprightly. Her movements stayed recorded in the soft undulations of the air as her waifish figure sailed from room to room before arriving in the kitchen to brew exotic teas. She would also hang makeshift billowing ethnic curtains that were later replaced by rich and thick fabrics. This was much later, after Adam had left the house to go to Toronto.

The porch used to be sloped and lovely. In the summer, the setting sun would hit it in the face. In the winter, while resisting the permanent drizzle, it looked like someone crying, quietly. The first floor had a vast and cold living room sparsely furnished with pieces that the many passersby had left behind: a La-Z-Boy, a sagging piano with distraught keys and rambunctious reverberation, and a handful of worn-out carpets and trinkets picked out from yard sales and back-alley bins. The dining room was dark and narrow, and for years it was only used to roll joints, drink Coronas, and play cards in a haze of thick smoke and bluegrass music. The kitchen was the soul of the entire building, and the fragrances from stews, tisanes, and baking rushed up the stairs all the way to the attic.

It was inevitable: Adam and Melanie were drawn to each other on that first day of June. The rain had stopped after many days, and humidity seeped up from the ground. There were flowers growing in disarray in the backyard, and there were greens budding in the vegetable garden, and the trees had begun to cast their shade all the way to the back alley. Melanie and Adam must have exchanged a few banal words about the greens and yellows, about the absence of rain and the signs of impending summer.

Facing the north front of the house, Melanie's room was the biggest. Her playful laugher bounced down the stairs when she found herself embracing Adam, breathing rapidly on his supple lips. They struggled sweetly at the top of the stairs on the second floor. Melanie pretended to flee to the third floor. The treacherously narrow and steep steps to the attic would only get her closer to Adam's room, the icebox, the coldest room in the house, without a heat vent, also facing north, right above Melanie's. Adam chased her upstairs, and when she tripped on the loose tenth step, he buried his face under her dress that had been infused with the aroma of peppermint from the garden. Precariously perched there on the steps, they jostled and cajoled each other, climbing one step and falling back two, until making it to the top and into the attic where they came together the way dreams dissolve in the gentle and slightly opiate early morning. The house's muscles abandoned all inhibition and caved in. Kisses and moans overflowed the sills and eves onto the sidewalk.

Once sated, their limbs remained intertwined and the cassette player played Leonard Cohen's "Famous Blue Raincoat." Melanie wanted to say something, but Adam, either afraid or enchanted, licked his index finger, and placed it on her lips and prevented any words from slipping through. He then slowly divided her in half all the way down to where she was moist and honeyed. It happened one more time, and even one more time, at the end of which they laid sprawled out on Melanie's bedroom floor, vibrating like hummingbirds. The sound of a third eye, a camera diaphragm, a shutter opening wide and closing in an impertinent blink barely disturbed their reverie. If they felt timid for a moment in their nakedness, it did not embarrass or annoy them much longer than that. Their curious silence was a subtle invitation for Kevin to step out from behind his camera, to sit by the bed, and, eventually, to join them. "Your pictures are so film noir," said Melanie with more allure than criticism in her tone. "It's about time that you lighten up." Melanie did not cover her breasts. The newcomer disrobed, timidly exposing powerful bodylines. For a moment, all three were mesmerized by their youth, and the huddle of embraces that ensued rolled across the bed like tumbleweeds of long vowels and dust.

For many weeks to come, the morning glory would mercilessly crawl and coil around the roses and the dahlias. Guided by the strange sounds like a whir from Melanie's throat, the two men would, at first, carefully arrange themselves to flank her, but after a while, all joined in a choreography that gave turns to Melanie and Adam to engulf Kevin's engorged silence. Kevin's conception of bodies as machines that could be repaired by using a scalpel began to change. And for Adam, this was a new and unique experience, painful at first, but deliriously pleasant after a short while. He craved the fitting of the bodies, the unrestrained struggle toward the little death. Melanie and Adam quickly seemed to come to an unspoken accord to cater to Kevin's every need and speed, to look after any crescent urge in his gleaming blue eyes, almost halogen, to entice his avid engine, and lap miles and miles of riding. Evenings would find them asleep like exhausted cubs, entangled in sleep.

Things began to drift by the end of the summer. Kevin, for one, seemed different, aloof, and less pliant to touch. Suddenly—or so it seemed—he stopped lending himself and his body to the many spontaneous provocations of his roommates, the tomfoolery under the kitchen table or the sensual larking about in the narrow hall upstairs. Adam and Melanie concurred that he was probably under a lot of stress. One fine day Kevin announced flatly that he had quit medical school—what Melanie had begun to describe as a "secure" future. Adam, piqued by Kevin's separation the last weeks, remarked that those sounded like Kevin's father's reproaches—"being the one who foots the tuition fees." The comment did not go over well. Kevin started some photography classes in a private institute. He spent his time away on a new motorbike, taking pictures, developing them in the rudimentary darkroom he had set up in the damp basement. When he was at home, he went around the house measuring the lights in the corners and the myriad ways in which they reflected on Melanie. The few times Adam was there, or interrupted, Kevin acted sullen and short-tempered. Untouchable. Melanie stayed out of the way whenever the two men barely exchanged a few words as they crossed paths in the kitchen. They would later discuss more in the basement, where there was also a washer and dryer. The racket of the old dryer would not let Melanie hear their words, and kept them from hearing Melanie with her morning sickness upstairs.

The end of summer left an odd man out; a terse conversation ensued after a bottle of *Dos Cuervos* had been drunk, after sex had stopped awkwardly. Maybe some stirring thoughts came upon Kevin's mind that made him quickly push Adam aside. Or was it that his new bicep tattoo of the Indian chief was too sore to the touch? Kevin scurried upstairs in the middle of a stream of oddly chosen words; things were said, and the house was momentarily filled with epithets and accusations that ricocheted off the walls like a poltergeist. A few hours later, when Adam tentatively descended the stairs in a dimmed light, Kevin stood behind Melanie who showed him the door with a stern index finger. It all unraveled as quickly as this. Adam left to go and clear his head. He did not intend to leave forever—he had little money and a predilection for crystal meth and late nights. He went to find Trinity for advice.

Adam was found naked near his third and last stop in Vancouver; the stop he made after visiting the house on

Woodland Drive, when the winds had began to blow inland from the ocean. Lying sideways, as if half-sitting on a bench off the Stanley Park bus loop, Adam's profile was placidly bathed by blood. A trembling hand fired up a cellphone at 5:00 a.m. — it was the dialing fingers of a young fussy homosexual on his way to work, stuffed into a designer shirt and tie, someone who did not appreciate the gentle smile that had petrified on Adam's lips, his gorgeous musculature reclining on one arm, his index finger, carefully stitched to his stump, extended upwards, gracefully, as if trying to touch the tip of a fatherly figure in the heavens above. He had regained his bearings and belongings — Adam had gone clear.

The sky streaked with gray announced the beginning of one long cloudy period for the city. Soon after being found, Adam's wounds were exposed to the obscene intermittent blue and red of ambulances and police cars, the hissing flashes from strangers' cameras, digitizing his pose, the macabre wink of diaphragms immortalizing this tableaux vivant before it was covered with a yellow plastic sheet — deemed not appropriate for general public viewing. One of the passersby, the gawkers, might have lingered a moment too long, holding his breath and his camera, but the police were too busy making annotations about "a grisly scene" to notice them. A few perfunctory phone calls were made later that day, before a distraught mother and a drag queen named Trinity would pick up the beautifully embalmed body from the coroner's and spirit it away to Penticton and into private oblivion.

Local newspapers showed their characteristic prudishness disguised as respect and barely reported the gory details. His name was summarily added to the growing list of killed or disappeared streetwalkers from the Downtown East Side — the Bermuda Triangle of junkies. No rallies were organized to protest his murder.

No one dared to say it might have been a misfortune of love. It looked like Adam had wandered naked through the park, the soles of his feet evidenced signs of that. It looked like he had been taken several times — there were traces of semen on him and drugs in his arteries.

As fate would have it, Kevin's twin brother, recently hired by the coroner's office and fresh from years of medical training, was the one who had to perform the autopsy. Such is life.

# ATONEMENT

*"A word is not a crystal, transparent and unchanged, it is the skin of a living thought..."*
*— Oliver Wendell Holmes*

"Place slices of raw beef, one at a time, between two sheets of plastic wrap and pound each slice with a flat mallet until the slices are very thin, approximately one eighth of an inch. Sprinkle freshly ground black pepper. Like revenge itself, carpaccio is best served chilled with bitter wedges of lemon."

The hostess of the show often chuckles at her own lame jokes. I got this recipe from one of those TV cooking shows, from the website attached to it actually. I'm not really in a position to cook myself, but I know a great deal about the procedure. Television plays an anesthetizing function. They keep it streaming in, seeping through the walls, with switches and dials to choose various options, except the option of not having it at all; that's not an option. They have TV monitors in every waiting room, airing cooking shows, talk shows, people showing off their old heirlooms like limp genitalia and getting a quote on how much it would cost on eBay. There are shows about medical procedures with little cameras like asps slithering through people's inners. They have replaced horror flicks with a daily flickering of misery, which has had the same effect on viewers as it had on Alex in *A Clockwork Orange* — numbness.

I adjust my headset and begin tapping on my keyboard. Media seems to have worked wonders for me too. It keeps me appeased. In this respect, Laura — the Borg mother — is very entrepreneurial. Kudos to her.

Today has been all about nothing, because little or

nothing happens in my world since I turned twenty—
nothing new that is. Whatever happens, happens mostly
in my head, and in this way I am not unlike many others.
Today we visited a specialist to get one of my Byzantine
orthopedic apparatuses to refine its futile function.
While they engaged in banal chatter about it, I mentally
edited a series of segments from gory movies. It is hard
to edit while my mother's platitudes play like a skipping
record. Don't they get tired of her playing noble mother?
The noble mother *scratch* the noble mother *scratch* noble
*scratch* mother *scratch* motherfucker. I "sample" Laura's
shrill bits and place them in a dismembered narrative:
Hannibal sautéing Ray Liotta's brains—gratuitous—and
then Lorena Bobbitt running through a windswept field,
cheating husband's cock held tight in her clenched fist,
raised up before her, thrown in the air not like a good
pitcher, but like a sissy. I put together Jeffrey Dahmer
and the pudgy boy from *Lord of the Flies*, and I make
them sing with k.d. lang dressed as St. Laura while she
elevates a bleeding heart in her cupped hands and
tenders it to the heavens above. St. Laura was a minor
saint thrown into a vat of molten lead by the Moors in
Spain in 864. I know a lot about scalding.

A BROTHER'S KEEPER IN NEARLY FATAL BLAZE
*The Daily Sentinel*, Kamloops, British Columbia
At 1:30 a.m. last night, a fire broke out in a house in
Lytton, in a developed basement where 14- and 17-
year-old brothers were sleeping. The boys' mother
and a relative were sleeping upstairs. When they were
awakened by the smoke in the house, they tried to get
down to the basement, but flames and smoke impeded
their access. The two women lived through intense
moments of panic as they were forced to stand
outside their house, watching the inferno flare out
from the lower level, and were unable to do anything
for the young men trapped inside.

By the time firefighters arrived, nearly ten minutes after the call, the younger brother had managed to drag his semiconscious older brother out into the yard through a basement window. Both suffered smoke inhalation and burns and were taken immediately to the local hospital. The fire was put out, but the house is likely to be condemned. An investigation into the cause of the fire will be conducted by the local police.

This morning, doctors at the Kamloops Hospital reported that both brothers are shaken but in stable condition. "It was a heroic act," said Laura L—, the mother of the two young men. "Axel is so small and frail, but he managed to save his brother's life." Axel's older brother—a promising hockey player for the local youth team—suffered third-degree burns over 60% of his body and cuts to his face. "The important thing is we are all alive, thank God," said their live-in relative as she consoled the distraught mother.

The only horrifying thing about media stories is their crass literal-mindedness and their factuality. A good story, because it is a lie, always keeps a secret. Back in my room, I can give myself over to the great small horrors of life: the fact that a priest, like my uncle George for example, can make wafer and wine transmogrify into the flesh and blood of a young victim, a solicitous God, a mysterious lamb spirit, an intricate trinity. I fire up search engines and look for information about carpaccio, because it seems normal under these conditions, like the cannibalism of Uruguayan rugby players stranded in the eternal Andean snows. It is the last resort. Why can't it be the first thing we think about? *Babette's Feast* and *Like Water for Chocolate*—what pushovers! Who fucking cares that people like them would fall in love with you because you cook well, really? I'd rather have *Eating*

*Raoul* or *Sweeney Todd*, or that big fat pansy Divine eating shit just to be in-your-face disgusting. It makes sense. We should eat our old and sick.

His awakening of my senses is overwhelming but delicate; it does not rush like thirst. It is the result of a season of slow craving; it is the burgeoning of seeds in a pod; it is a lukewarm vehicle of subtle fragrance and immense vulnerability. It is a flower—soft petal, pistil and stamen—that fears the miscarriage of a dull season, the lack of sun, or inversely, a deluge of rays. The awakening of my senses begins with the swelling of minutes like ripening grapes, lengthening until I ache. It begins when I suspect that Axel might be walking sure-footedly in my direction, approaching the corner, entering the house, led in by my mother (the stoic Laura), stepping softly inside, and shifting the wooden structure of the house slightly. There will be a series of creaks as the backbone of the house settles under his weight. A house that lies down and offers itself for the awakening. Axel might be saying good morning to Laura in a whisper, asking "How is he?"—meaning whether this is a good time to see me or not. My awakening is the approach of his ghost down the corridor to where my room is.

"The soul selects her own society," wrote Emily Dickinson in her self-confinement, "then shuts the door..." I quickly right-click on the mouse and close down screen windows as Axel looms over the threshold—he can't hear the robotic "minimize" sound scheme because I have the earpiece in. Sometimes Axel is all hands, like translucent dust gently blowing across the room and making the curtains sway. Sometimes he feels like the powerful presense of the world at my doorstep. His ruddy hands can open my cocoon to offer me to the sunlight. The scent of moving parts emanates from his palms and under his nails. He quietly presses on my face, my hand, and my thigh, where he leaves a faint imprint. His words tell me the daily goings on, are alive, and crawl inch by inch along my skin seeking the shelter of an orifice. Once the words and I get past the initial bitter pain of contact, they start whispering, making me love, and making love to me.

Axel often comes to visit after a 10K on his days off. He casually exchanges his damp running gear for jeans and a T-shirt while he talks to me. His clothes smell of traffic and noise, commerce and trading, they exude a hint of women in fitted two-piece suits, and of Axel's desire treading behind them. His needs exude all around his muscles like a watermark. I register his every perception, his every insight. I keep them alive until the next visit (while my third eye above my monitor digitizes his every move). He tells me about a night out in the pub with some buddies, a strained phone conversation with his ex-wife, and I feel the pouring of beer and the surcharge of testosterone. A few measured questions and Axel unravels—the hours and the sowing of seeds. Come on, Axel, hand those thoughts over so I can skin them alive. Tell me more about last night. And he begins to recount—Laura knocks quietly at the door, and my heart halts!

Laura knows when to enter, when to exit. Her sense of timing has refined itself over the years, since the moment our father left us and her process of beatification accelerated: from a pudgy housewife with flat feet—too tall for a descendant of poor Calabrese peasants—and a two-bit Catholic from a small and dried-up interior town into St. Laura, the Borg virgin. It is uncanny how she knows how to attend to even my darkest bodily functions, how she keeps an invisible cordon around Axel's motives, and how she discreetly knocks at a closed door before any consummation might occur. Laura often whispers to Axel her concerns about me. I can hear them *in camera*. My domains are expansive, and I can keep track of a great deal. I can surmise the ebbs and flows of their lives by the gradations and inflections in their voices, the patterns of their movements, their pulses. (They have tried to get me out, to socialize, to be with others, to live a "different" life—haven't I single-handedly brought enough prosperity to their lives? The charity and experimental treatments. The government subsidies for the disabled.) My computer's memory, powerful as it is—updated often to comply with my demands for progress—merely keeps up. It helps me to seek, review, and archive details, card numbers, charges, license plates, charts, and prescriptions; it gnaws relentlessly like a rat. The sun never rises in my digital empire.

Things happen to Axel that he doesn't fully understand—not all the time, but they do. He gets caught committing adultery, though it seemed there was *no way* it could be found out, particularly as it happened under the auspices of Laura, under the protective roof of the ancestral home. Laura's wish to have another child at her disposal, a fully functional one, does not pan out, and the day nurse, buxom and tight, has to be dismissed—Pity! Later that year, Axel breaks his arm playing hockey just when he is ready to relocate to Vancouver Island to take a well-paying paramedic job, and he has to stay. Laura begins to show signs of anxiety about seeing Axel go and having to stay here stuck with me. There are little pearls of sweat glistening on her forehead, like a translucent halo, as she studiously explains "things to come" to the retard. It is I who am in sheer terror, like James Caan in *Misery*, fearing that she might start breaking my delicate instruments, might wreck my voice-activated mouse, my compass to the world, or might disconnect my cable modem, my umbilical cord, anything to keep Axel in town.

The day Axel came to announce he intended to move to Vancouver Island, something burned up inside of me as if I had been left bare under sunlight. He said this was his "big chance," now that he didn't have a wife at home—the "girl" that Laura could not control, hard as she had tried with a governess' stiff-upper-lip smile. That day we came very close. Axel's touch was anxious but lasting. In it, I could measure the strength of his muscles, the tension in his ligaments, and the wattage putting them in motion. He had stopped by after his run, and his heart seemed ready to be harvested and transplanted into a virgin chest. I was open and offering, waiting for his hands to come and deliver. He leaned over me longer than usual. Gently, he talked about our good times—no mention of the bad times—and talked about "our future." He caressed the tip of my earlobe while words of hope and love, near and far, home, hearth, and mother, of going away trickled in.

His bittersweet struggle made me nauseous. Pity and worry for me, mixed with lust for distance from me, slid through his lips, so close to mine, closer than ever, all to tell me he was releasing me into the vast dark of this house with the ghost of Laura shuffling about. I rejected his cheating heart, and the taste of his blood turned back into acidic wine. Two-faced motherfucking bastard! I wished him luck with a curved smile. He didn't stay long; he collected his damp clothes; he said goodbye, softly, before his heavy feet stomped down the stairs; and after a while, I heard the front door close. Off he went to celebrate, watch some hockey, down a couple of beers, and meet his second girlfriend this year. (The other had not fully packed up her things from his apartment. I knew. Online, I could check the telephone bills, and the comings and goings through the alarm company.) Once I regained control of my pulse and overcame the aches of my body, I searched the Internet, emailed friends, my invisible covenant, and my virtual archivists swiftly perused a thousand files like the freaky but dedicated monks in *The Name of the Rose*. My voice trembled so badly at times that I had a hard time activating the voice recognition feature on my system. By seven, I vomited Laura's bland food onto her arthritic hands. I stayed awake until midnight listening to the wolves howl.

It is odd how things turn out. As we grew up, he was younger, always sickish, thin as a limp tree branch, and painfully bashful. At eighteen, a few months shy of getting into college on a sports scholarship, I was destined to be written up in the yearbook as the one "most likely to be a college jock." The girls said it all the time, giggling, looking at my figure. They said mischievously that I was a daredevil dynamo; they said, in whispers, that I was a hunk. They snuck peeks at the bulge in my pants. To tell the truth, I had a carnivorous appetite, for life, for everything. Axel inherited it—as Laura always says to whoever wants to hear it—along with the rugged frame of a hockey player chiseled by a million daredevil stunts. A small scar crosses the lower section of his left chin. The hair on the nape of his neck is as thick as a brush. He has a square jaw and square shoulders and two crooked fingers, the index and the thumb, which possess an extraordinary permutation of command and tenderness. He's always dreamed of being a paramedic—to help others, as he says, sounding like a beauty contest runner-up. That is exactly what he became: a saviour—to frequently slake that thirst of guilt and envy that sane and healthy people have. Funny how things turned out that summer in Reno in our shoddy motel room. We had so much fun going to Hope, then to Vancouver, a gargantuan metropolis in our eyes, to catch a Greyhound; even when Laura spent a lot of time fussing over Axel's motion sickness and lack of appetite for big American portions. My aunt Beverly was her usual absentminded fool, lost mostly in the stridence of tickling coins, tokens, or diving into the watered-down free drinks—my mother mumbled that she behaved "exactly like your father had" almost a decade before. I vaguely remembered him; Axel didn't. Beverly lost loads of money. It didn't matter much; we were there for only two more days, and it was all so exciting. After that, we would head back to rural British Columbia and a long dry winter—it turned out to be a brittle dry winter; everything was dry and brittle that year. Forest fires erupted all over the place; houses and trees burned like candlelight.

Our room in Reno was stuffy, the way mine gets in the summertime here, stagnant, and damp. My mother and aunt Beverly went down to the San Remo bar for a nightcap. We had an early dinner with loads of gravy and mayonnaise on various fried meats. Axel hadn't been feeling well and seemed morose and ready to hit the sack. I watched a *Dukes of Hazzard* rerun on a fading TV screen, then flicked through the other channels, even adult movies (we didn't figure out they were instantly being charged to our room—it was the novelty of it all). Axel perked up; he didn't look that sick to me. We didn't talk a lot, not then, not ever. He sometimes asked questions, stupid questions to which I would reply with stupid answers. Do you want to smoke? Have you smoked weed? What is a hooker? What happens if you put Tiger Balm on the tip of your cock? He was sort of obnoxious that way. He was only fourteen.

He approached me. I saw him out of the corner of my eye, the way I sense his presence at my door even now, almost gently, like a serpent. I swatted him on the head—What difference does it make whether I resisted? But I did, to no avail—we wrestled, horsed around a bit, but after a while his body was inseparable from mine. He was focused and constant and felt viscous and slippery to the very end, in the very darkness. The room swayed and twirled; the ceiling was flat and covered with the grime of tobacco smoke; my awakening was like a gushing wound.

I have been under siege since that night. My body has been under siege since that night. My senses betrayed me and kidnapped me; this is why I don't feel any other attachment to this carcass than the most functional. I am the caretaker of a condemned building. On the trip back, I was silent, thinking how I would break the strange news to Laura (my aunt drank too much to notice anything). I'd heard about this before, in hockey practice; my buddies and I made jokes about it. I'd gone through hazing when I joined the team, the elephant walk. I'd never imagined this would happen to me. Many times, I'd wished, intensely, I would wake up from this nightmare. Wake up to my delicious experimentation with Shirley, my girlfriend then—a bit of taunting, a bit of second base, a bit of pot, a bit of having it, her, bit by bit. Instead, I came to in the fire, singeing and searing away all those forbidden memories that had been sweetly grafted over my skin: us raising hell, the damnation of St. Laura, secretly; the exquisite pastimes that became great and intimate feats of prowess and bonding; welding ourselves together late into the evening, or in the midday with the sun piercing my eyes. How could I ever look at the sun again? Axel and I ought to have remained melted together. Lord knows I tried to drag him down, fighting him every inch of our way out of those basement windows.

Desire, when stoked by fear, is like teeth clenching on

supple tissue. Arsonists of the heart, we allowed the fire to propagate; we stoked the flames, mesmerized by the blaze in our eyes and on our skin. We would seek out occasions, often, to solicit energy and to bend our pride, that is how we understood it, as an affront—our closeness came in the battle, that is the only way we could conceive of such desire. There was no possible way out, no window of opportunity. There was no explanation for what I would be surely be blamed for; I was the eldest, the strongest. It lasted the length of summer and long into fall and winter—without discontent but replete with the feelings that were Laura's wretched trinity: fear, ignorance, and secrecy.

After the house fire, I was finally left alone to drown slowly in their pity. Machines crawled and whirred and probed and scratched layers of deep tissue with fistulas, catheters, clamps, twisters, tacks; an arsenal of appliances were grafted to me. Cauterized, harvested, and implanted, some kind of freedom came upon me. There is space for freedom even when pity and yearning and envy and anger all are tied around me like the barbs on a wire of metallic rhythms. I learned that people wish upon themselves all manner of accidents and tragedies and disgust and any other epic things that can make their dull souls vibrate. No one can moderate the slow torture of singed flesh, flayed in grafting, transported in slices by white muses and industrial operators from one aseptic region of my body to the other, to be replanted like spikes under my nails, the industrial processing of live flesh. I read Dante's words:

> Pausing in his savage meal / the sinner raised his mouth and wiped it clean along the hair left on his head whose back he had laid waste / Then he began / "You asked me to endure reliving a grief so desperate / even the thought

torments my heart even as I prepare to tell it /
But if my words are seeds / with fruit of infamy
for this traitor that I gnaw / I will both speak
and weep within your sight."

Torture is not possible without an adoring audience.

How else could I have kept Axel around? How else
could I survive Laura's smothering? Someone had to go
to create more need, and poor old drunk Beverly seemed
so perfectly poised to see her maker, to set the stage for
more ties that bind. Her passing right as Axel was
making noises about leaving us was momentous. There
were some quieter times after Beverly's funeral, and
some ghost of serenity staked out our house. But, of
course, his voracity had to go and find more fire, and
after a short period of dating Axel got married to that
fine Alberta nitwit with the curved lips. And then I had
to gift a version of our family history to the dazzling
bride, straight from *my* curved lips. Although the words
I pronounced were recognizable, the tone and bearer of
such speech were not. Like my face, I digitally distorted
the anonymous recording that was delivered to her
doorstep on the day of her wedding. I wasn't there, but I
can almost hear her bewildered tone, redolent of biblical
wonder. I saw her eyes bulging in their wedding
portraits. They reminded me of Shirley's the last time I
talked to her, after I was brought back from the intensive
care unit to "the new house" Laura had diligently
secured for us through a process of prurient public
appeal. How else could I have stopped them both,
Shirley and the Alberta nitwit, from birthing Axel
children and walking away with him into a candy
sunset? Who wouldn't try to elope with Axel? as Laura
eloquently put it to anyone who would listen. She was in
on my actions, she always has been, the fucking coward,
but forever cloaked in her victimhood.

Summer is winding down, but it's been an inferno. There are wildfires erupting like tongues of fire all over the land, some near our house. Many times Axel has had to come because they have imposed an evacuation alert, and I might have to be taken out of the house and the expensive equipment salvaged; the fire is too close. And then, the wind stops, and the planes drench everything with their heavy cloud of red smoke. Laura struggles day and night—I wonder if she closes her eyes at night. I don't. It's my favorite time. She superstitiously tries to stave off the nearing fire by sheer prayer. She resists the theories of careless tourists throwing cigarette butts out their car windows on the Trans-Canada Highway or Highway 12 as proposed by *The Daily Sentinel*. She says little, but she looks at me with deeply entrenched distrust when she changes my tubular compression garments twice a day. She may be thinking how could the fire have caressed the ground so closely to where she stood, as if it had originated there, as if she would self-combust and burn like the virgin whose name she carries like a curse. Her mousy little eyes, lost in her dignified countenance, betray her thoughts. Last Tuesday, when Axel came over, I could hear her contained breathing behind the door, just as she could hear our contained breathing inside. It was Axel's turn to do my care, change the bandages, attending to my body's largest organ, mangled but alive. Looking at us from the outside is like seeing a strange lopsided cathedral triptych divided by a door. And so we live, in a profound trinity of inspired thoughts, never spoken, veiled but melded together like the allografting of skins, the two brothers in here, sharing our room, sharing one epidermis, while Laura, the saint, who lives to make our home our prison, who dresses our wounds, stands out there, sharing the moment at a distance. I am the fuel that ignites everlastingly our burning lamp. No one will leave this sacred house of love.

# MOUNTAIN DEW

In 1993 many brand new condo buildings constructed in the late 1980s around Greater Vancouver in British Columbia began to show signs of leakage and deterioration due to poor construction standards, faulty materials, and cost cutting on the part of unscrupulous contractors. This has caused great distress to many new homeowners who have chosen Vancouver as their home for its majestic location against a maze of mountains covered with virgin forests. In the past years, we have heard sad and even bizarre stories of broken hearts and bank accounts and grueling repair work.

*News Items Magazine*,
Vancouver, British Columbia, 2001

With one exact gesture, a blue tie briskly uncoils from under Bruce's crisp blue shirt collar. He unbuttons the shirt, one by one, and disrobes to reveal to the large bare window his solid chest wrapped in a skintight CK microfiber white tank top. After a second thought, he draws the blinds, quickly, with a sure, brawny hand; the evening is winding down out there; a dark cumulus suffuses the sky with gray. Ross' hands glide from behind, counting Bruce's distinct ridges: one, two, three, four—almost a six-pack.

Bruce pulls away from him.

"Not now," he says and begins to take off his blue pants. He carefully finds the sharp ironed middle line and runs it between his index finger and thumb, folds the pants over, and hangs them on the cedar valet at the end of his queen-size bed to keep them wrinkle-free. The bedroom is not far from the kitchen or from the living room in this large studio, but the few stark and serviceable fixtures make it look spacious. Ross purses his full lips, and a blond curl falls over his forehead. Sulking, he looks down and fidgets with the worn-out Whistler Mountain day-pass tag fastened to the end of his red Gortex jacket.

"You know, my *interest* sort of...well, during the workweek." Bruce dismisses Ross' pouting and changes the topic: "How was your day, anyway?" Ross shrugs his shoulders and grimaces as he tries to conjure up one remarkable event from the mountain slopes — it has all been the usual daredevil slaloms and deep sweeps.

Oblivious, Bruce continues, "I missed my training session today. Steven will be upset. He wanted to start me on a new workout circuit." He pauses to peel off his socks and underwear and place them in the laundry hamper conveniently hidden inside a mirrored closet. "A good workout invigorates me." Bruce, now resolutely naked, inspects his body's outline in the full mirror.

Ross has given up standing in the middle of the room. His hands fumble to find two boxes of Lean Cuisine in the freezer. Once he has pulled one corner of the plastic wrap up — a domestic lesson he has never forgotten since three minor implosions — he pops them into the microwave. Then he takes his Gortex off, hangs it up in the closet by the door, kicks his shoes off, and puts them by the door in alignment with Bruce's spit-shined regulation black boots.

Bruce points at Ross. "Take it all off." Ross reveals all 190 lbs and 6'2" of his strapping twentysomething figure, and his tiny dick salutes. "Stay," Bruce says, and Ross complies.

Later, sitting across from each other at the stainless-steel kitchen counter, they look like two dutiful children eating in a school cafeteria. Ross carries on trying to make chit-chat (like the small cartoon dog that continually jumps around the big dog yelping, "Hey, Chester! Wow, Chester! How do you like that, Chester?"). "How is your new co-worker? Do you call each other 'partners'? It's a woman, right? How's that for you?" Undisturbed, Bruce transports small pieces of chicken cacciatore and wild rice from the disposable container to his mouth without missing a grain. This evening, like the one before and the one that will follow, every domestic detail will occur in its rightful place at the right time. But unlike the other days, today, in an hour, Bruce will be handing Ross a brochure for a sex addicts anonymous group that meets on Tuesday nights at the United Church in the West End. This is the end; this is goodbye.

One week later, on Tuesday evening...

"What on earth...!" Bruce pulls a gray Nike sweatshirt over his head and storms out of the apartment, climbs up the stairs two and three steps at a time. Politely at first, he knocks at the door of the apartment above, but he has to repeat this, louder, without losing his composure. On the other side, Ella Fitzgerald croons "Stormy Weather"; he recognizes the song because his father used to play it. The door opens wide.

"Hi, come in!" invites a pudgy and slightly bemused man in his fifties, his voice sounding surprisingly familiar. He has no neck and a double chin, and his housecoat barely covers his scraggly belly.

"No thanks," Bruce says coolly while holding the man's mousy gaze. He notices the music is now turned down and then a lanky naked figure zips past to the bathroom at the left of the main door. In passing, he quickly glances Bruce's way.

"Your music is too loud. It is already 7:30 and...the banging...the banging is...well..." In a lower tone, Bruce amends his complaint with a "you *know* what I am referring to."

"Certainly. I'm sorry. I didn't notice. I was taking a shower." The editor looks drenched under that housecoat. "Sure you don't want to come in? We'll be grabbing a bite." "No thanks," Bruce mutters as he turns around, mortified. He realizes that in his rush to go upstairs he is wearing only a sweatshirt and a crisp pair of Banana Republic boxer shorts. As Bruce flees, the chubby man continues to blabber. "We—I will turn down the music. I have work to do—what's your name?" But Bruce is already down the stairs. He can't get away quick enough. "I work as an editor for a GLBTQ rag..." The man loudly spells out the acronym, and it reverberates down the stairs after Bruce.

Later that year, in his Discharge Report to Correctional Services, Bruce will carefully describe the noise upstairs as being "similar to the trampling of horses and loud songs." And although he tosses and turns until late that night, he doesn't go back upstairs to the editor's suite to complain.

A crisp fall wind laps at their faces through the open window. Bruce drives the institutional vehicle conscientiously, arms in a ten-to-two position.

"Often, I come back from my evening workout, I have my dinner, and I have to put up with *the* noise," Bruce complains. "I've explained it to him—this editor upstairs—how their noise travels down through our building."

His colleague half smiles. "Don't you ever make noise yourself? I mean you and..." Bruce stiffens, uncomfortably, as he hangs a sharp right corner to head downtown.

"Some things are private."

"Some noises are public." Connie takes one wicked look at him through the corner of her eye. They come to a full stop at the traffic lights, and their attention is caught by a couple of grungy teenagers in black T-shirts and torn baggy black jeans studded with metal spikes. They are standing in the middle of the road. They carry their skateboards strapped across their backs as if they were pieces of urban body armor. The youngsters ambush the first two cars, wielding sodden squeegees. The Corrections Canada vehicle becomes an immediate target.

"Hey. No, no. Don't." Bruce tries to dissuade a young guy from his guerrilla attack with exasperated hand gestures. "Can't you see it's a government car? You idiot!" But the windshield wipers have already been pulled back, and the window is covered with soap sludge.

"C'mon, Bruce," she says, "give him something." She digs in her pockets looking for Loonies.

Bruce frowns. Three more skillful slashes across the windshield take most of the muddy water away, leaving a hazy film all over the windshield; on the double, the boy turns to the driver's window. Bruce is caught in the knife-like slant of a pair of emerald eyes, almost iridescent.

Befuddled, Bruce blurts out, "This is illegal," and takes from the boy's outstretched hand the money that his colleague has given him. The raspy touch of slender, cold, dirt-under-the-nails fingers trying to retrieve the coins startles him.

"Oh, Bruce, get over it." Connie grabs the coins from him and deposits them back in the boy's extended palm.

Bruce huffs, shifts to second, steps on the gas, and lurches past the grinning figure.

"I've seen those guys hanging out there before. I should report them." He spits these lines.

"These kids sure get you going, don't they?" They are entering the Correctional Services parking lot, and Bruce pretends not to hear her remark. He hops out, checks his pants looking for creases, shuts the door, and as they walk into the building continues as if nothing had interrupted their conversation five minutes earlier. "In any case, I will have to talk to him again—this so-called 'editor,' I mean—seriously. My plumbing problem in the bathroom originates upstairs. Why am I not surprised?"

That evening Bruce calmly goes about his routine. He sharply presses PLAY on the answering machine and begins to disrobe, tie-first, as always. A piercing beep is followed by a message, "Bruce? Hi, Ross here. Sorry, I'm not going to be able to make it today. I mean I have to write midterms, and I am going to...um, that new support group you recommended—you know, the codependent anonymous one." Another piercing beep. The next message is from Bruce's mother telling him to show up punctually at church on Saturday because his Auntie Claire will be doing one of the readings. The last message plays, an airy voice struggling to thread the words together. "Bruce, hi, it's me, Connie. Didn't want to talk about this at work. I know what you think about on-duty hours." She gives off an apologetic snigger. "Anyway, like you told me, I'm trying, but...the other day in the parking lot, a lot really changed for me...I mean, that book you gave me after...it really changed things for me...thanks. I haven't been...*out* to a bar for three evenings in a row, and I—" The machine gives this hesitant caller the hook exactly after one minute, as per Bruce's laconic digital greeting: "Be brief and to the point."

Later that same evening, Bruce, reenergized by several rounds of squats and abs, takes a long deep breath and hikes up the stairs. He knocks. After a minute, the door opens but not as wide as usual; it opens only a crack, enough to reveal a pair of curious green eyes that check him out from head to toe. Softly, Nina Simone's "Wild is the Wind" leaks out.

Bruce is uncharacteristically stumped, at a loss for words. "Is...um...," he's forgotten his name, "...the 'editor' here?"

"Nah."

"Will he be back soon?" Now Bruce's voice sounds strained.

"Uh-uh."

"Will you tell him that I need to talk to him?" Bruce hesitates for an instant. "In fact, I have asked a plumber here tomorrow morning to check this, er, your bathroom, to see about that leak. I hope that will be okay with you...with you two."

"Yup."

"The plumber will be here at around ten." The door closes gently as Bruce completes his sentence.

The remedy of the plumber, at least for the best part of an hour, between ten and eleven the next morning, seems worse than the ailment of the leak. There is loud banging upstairs, then something like loud voices, and then more banging. Bruce tries to hide his irked mood while he apologizes perfunctorily to his mother for sleeping in and not showing up at church this morning. The cellphone somewhere in his jacket keeps ringing too. Once he manages to deflate his mother's dreary sermon—a perfect use of his conflict resolution training at work—Bruce marches upstairs to see for himself what the ruckus is all about.

He motions to knock at the door, but it is not locked, and with a slight push, it opens. Janis Joplin and the scratching of a needle into the grooves of spinning vinyl blare from the speakers. Out of the bathroom comes a sonorous thump—not hammering or drilling—*thump, thump*. Bruce walks in to find two steel-toe Caterpillar boots in the air, perched on a young man's wide shoulders. The plumber is moaning, getting ferociously pounded between the toilet and the sink stand. Janis howls, "Take another little piece of my heart..." A series of knee-jerk reactions takes place: the plumber peeks over her companion's shoulder and sees Bruce; she quickly disengages herself, and jumps to her feet, exposed and sweaty; she frantically pulls up her Dickies and collects herself; the young naked man, drenched in sweat, slowly turns around on one knee, one sly hand resting on the other, panting, and wearing a rapacious grin beneath his wide green eyes.

Bruce will devote more than one line in his discharge report to *those* wide eyes he characterizes as "Eurasian" and to the apparently disturbing effect they have on him. He will recount having immediately abandoned the apartment to go downstairs "to collect himself and think clearly of a possible course of action." Actually, what happens is that Bruce and the plumber stumble into each other as they walk out the front door at the same time. Later, Bruce does not complain about this incident to the building manager. He opts for what he will report as an "even-keeled approach that would give his neighbors a chance to explain themselves." Once he realizes such an explanation will not be provided anytime soon, he calls upstairs at an "appropriate" time to have a formal conversation with the "editor."

"Bruce, believe me, I appreciate your discretion. The kid is a guest, and he means no harm. His hormones are raging, but he meant no harm. He's a distant relative; he'll be gone soon. In fact, he's spent the last two nights at a friend's place." The editor catches his troubled breath. "Bruce, you are a man of the law...well, I mean, given *your* line of work. I am sure that you appreciate that at my age—not to mention in *my* line of work, which is not what one would call alluring—one does have to be, shall I say, *creative* about life options. We sometimes engage in..."

Bruce stands up as if a firecracker has exploded in his pants, flashes on a memory of his reservist years, clicks his heels, and abruptly bids the editor farewell before heading out.

"Sorry, getting those Janis Joplin records was my idea. He mostly likes classic blues and jazz and..." The rest of the editor's non sequitur explanation is brutally silenced by the slamming of the front door.

"Hey dude! You've been watchin' me at the corner, right?" The nearness of his voice startles Bruce. He quickly looks to his right and left and takes a few steps to the far side of the south building where he cannot be as easily seen with the squeegee boy, who, in the afternoon drizzle, resembles a pitiful Robin Hood.

"Turn that down." Bruce points to the kid's earphones that vibrate with Klaus Nomi's impossible high Cs.

"Cool, eh?" His translucent and dilated emerald eyes calmly come to rest on Bruce's crisply turned out figure. "Why you so interested in me?" He pauses and takes a long guzzle of Mountain Dew from a one-liter bottle. "Don't want you fuckin' around with the editor. Don't fuck 'round with the editor. Hear me?" His breath is close enough to fog up Bruce's thinly rimmed Armani spectacles. "He doesn't ask for much, not much, even if it sometimes leaks down. And I get a pad to crash." Bruce's lips are tight, his fists are tight, and the hairs on the back of his neck have risen.

"That blond guy, the snowboarder, he roams around the building at night, you know? Sly muthafucka, that is. Watch out. He's out to get you, that muthafucka." The wet air is blue, and his tone flushed with something like an invitation to wrestle.

"How do you know that?" asks Bruce, cold as a blade.

"Seen him on MTV. Won a fuckin' snowboarding medal or something, right?" He lets out a hoarse chuckle. "A pothead, he is."

"I don't have the slightest idea of what you are talking about. Anyway, I will present a complaint to the Strata Council and see that you and the editor are asked to vacate these premises, permanently." Bruce is indignant. "Or I will have to contact the appropriate authorities."

"What! You're gonna call the fuckin' *police*? Fuck man, how goes it? People who have glass ceilings... something or other." The squeegee boy's voice has lowered to a sardonic rasp.

"What do you mean?"

"No sweat, dude. I'm cool. Lots of guys come to see me at the corner. They want this or that. I'm cool."

Twilight dims in the boy's eyes. He turns to the wall and takes a long leak; a warm steam rises between his body and the wall. Casually, he adds, "West side, well-to-do dudes, fancy bitches, know shit about *making whoopee*, man, you see. Or that flat Connie chick you banged in the parking lot a couple of weeks ago. They know fuck all. *I* , on the other hand, can give you a mean ride if —" He doesn't end his offer. Bruce grabs him by a fistful of jet black hair and pulls his head back. The drizzle now soaks his face like tears.

"Yes...sir?" the kid mutters provocatively. "Leave your apartment door open some night, and you'll see what I mean."

Enfuriated, Bruce pushes him off, and the kid's forehead strikes the grainy wall. The squeegee boy retreats but turns once more to glance wild-eyed over his shoulders. He wears his sly smile again, a streak of blood trickling down from the gash in his long thin eyebrow and blending with the raindrops around his lovely mouth. A second later he throws the empty Mountain Dew bottle at Bruce's feet, skillfully drops his skateboard, hops on it, and propels himself around the corner. Bruce's shaken hand picks up the empty bottle. He will later place it in a blue recycling bin.

In his report Bruce will maintain that this has been a case of "homosexual panic," and he will recant having uttered any threats, and from having caused any bodily harm to the boy. Bruce's impeccable record will be kept intact to accommodate a last-minute request from his superior, who will state, in a separate document, that Bruce probably acted on "a blind basic instinct." His discharge papers will list "extenuating circumstances" as one of the main causes for his early retirement.

Thursday, late afternoon. Bruce comes home early to wait for a Thanksgiving package from his Auntie Claire. It has been over a week since Bruce told the editor that the squeegee boy had to leave. Upstairs, Peggy Lee is deliriously singing out "Fever" — and very, very loudly. It leaks down into Bruce's flat.

A tentative voice comes out of the answering machine — always turned up to full volume — to deliver a quick despondent message: "Hey, Bruce, please. I need to see you. I've been going to meetings as I promised."

Abruptly, Bruce tells the UPS guy to dismount him. "You'd better get going. That's my girlfriend."

"Sounds like a man to me." UPS circumspectly removes an extra-large Trojan. In a quasi-military tone Bruce commands, "No, don't throw it in here" — and hands the brown guy a paper towel like a doctor handing out a tissue after an anal probe — "throw it in the basket in the bathroom."

UPS rolls his eyes. "Don't like not finishing what I start, man," he spits out as he pulls up his tight brown pants.

"Finish! You...went *soft* on me. Listen, finish your delivery now."

"It's the noise from above, man. It distracts me."

"Long dick, short attention span," Bruce mutters as the willowy bearer of nine thick UPS inches disappears into the bathroom for a minute.

"Your ceiling is leaking," UPS announces as he comes out, rearranging himself. He picks up his automated flip chart and indicates, "Sign here, please." Bruce complies and sees him to the door, where he hands him a card for a sex addicts anonymous group.

UPS pockets it with disdain. "Whatever."

It is getting dark when Bruce, after scrubbing himself pink with pHisoderm under a scalding shower, walks up one flight of stairs, then retraces his steps, then turns to go up again. Like this, stepping up and then down, he makes it once more to the fourth floor. His clammy grip turns the knob, and he steps into a candlelit room where outlines and shadows are suspended in midair, air heavy with the aroma of weed. The bathroom door frames a bizarre tableau: sitting at the toilet, a life-size Buddha, bathed in the glow of a golden shower, holds a beatific grin. At times, the Buddha opens his mouth wide to collect the generous golden liquid and perform a gleeful ablution. One flabby hand rests on his knee and holds a pink denture, the other rests on the other knee and holds a small amber bottle. The steam from the running hot water wasting away in the bathtub lingers like an effluvium. The nerve endings in Bruce's bare feet are electrified on the wet bathroom tile floor.

A small Chinese postman looks like a comic-book superhero who might be lifted airborne by his bright yellow rubber rain cape. He dodges the puddles as he scurries into the Capilano Rooms. The busy reception area smells of filth and urine. With his small hands, he swats away the junkies that besiege him like mosquitoes and drops a bundle of government-issued brown envelopes at the attendant's window. The lucky ones get their checks sent; the rest will have to shuffle to the nearby social services office, fittingly numbered Hastings 666. Welfare Wednesday unfolds like a nine-ring circus every last Wednesday of the month with junkies and whores gyrating on the corners like kamikaze trapeze artists and zany jugglers. Later that morning, the Capilano Rooms attendant knocks loudly on the door of one of the stingy rooms at the end of a dark corridor. When the door opens, he hands the occupant an anonymous note that reads: "Please come back. I will do anything to have you near me again."

When called to answer questions at the Correctional Services Centre, the Capilano Rooms attendant will declare to have seen only the lanky figure of the squeegee boy cloaked in a red Gortex jacket.

"Fuck if *I* know! You know 'em junkies. They just lie 'bout, doin' nothin'. For all I know, he ripped it off someone." He swore he never saw a "decent" blond in the room, male or female. "I'm telling ya, there are no visitors allowed, *ever*."

Uncomfortably, Bruce pieces together a conversation he has with the editor in which he delivered an ultimatum. This conversation takes place about two months before the pleading note is delivered at the Capilano Rooms, only weeks after witnessing what Bruce describes as an "apparition" in the editor's bathroom. At this time, Bruce, who looks somewhat unhinged, states, "It is essential for me to get eight hours of sleep." Reportedly, the editor responds, "You must be a Libra, someone who finds bliss in domestic harmony," which is followed by a "Not to worry. I'll look into the matter." They briefly sit down to talk, at Bruce's request—both of them will clearly remember that — and that the squeegee boy is not present.

"I want to get this kid out of 'the life.' I mean dodging cars and cleaning windshields in the rain for quarters and loonies. It's kind of, you know, absurd. I think he should work as an escort, or in a massage parlor." The editor lights up another cigarette.

Bruce's lips do not move; they form a livid thick line. When he curves them, his tone is restrained and flattened. "Absurd! Your idea of helping this individual is to have him turn tricks for a living! Where is the dignity in that? I should report *you*."

"How much do you make a month?"

"What!" Exasperation taints Bruce's voice.

"I mean how much can a boy with no education, no money, no family, with nothing but a checkered past as a foster child that is too traumatic for you to believe it's real, what can he aspire to make in a month? Where? At McDonald's? Have you seen the octogenarians who work at McDonald's? How dignified is *that*?"

"You should speak of dignity!" Bruce is on his feet, towering over the editor. "Listen, it is not my concern what kinds of choices he makes — or what choices *you* make. The point here is that he has to find another place to live, or I will have to talk to the landlord and the police." With sure feet he strides to his door and opens it to signal a dismissal. As the editor waddles his way out, Bruce adds, "If you care for him so much, why don't you...keep him?"

The editor replies unexpectedly in the low sweet voice of a concerned father. "I would, in the blink of an eye, if I could, but I don't have the means. My fifteen minutes of publishing glory are up. I can't keep beauty in a cage when there is such a wide world out there in which he deserves to live. And I can't blame him for wanting it either." Bruce hands him a government-issued brochure. It is about a support group for "street-involved" kids. Then he slowly closes the door but does not lock the deadbolt.

Debbie will testify that whatever problems she may have had when she began the day, she did not discourage young, handsome, and intelligent clients from getting "Hired Hands" services. Her philosophy is that "beauty and youth are the worst enemies of a client-driven business." She will explain that she has more problems with the "Paris Place" *masseuses*—abusive pimps, drugs, faulty hair extensions and nails, staggering needs for counseling on age-angst, pregnancy, and diseases—than with the "Hired Hands" *masseurs*. She will pepper her account with dutiful asides about health standards and good service and accompanies it with subtle but effective hand gestures. In a compassionate tone, which is either entirely hypocritical or profoundly sincere, she will recall waiting in her small stuffy office and deliberating on whether or not to approach this case "as a cold business woman, or in a more stern, motherlike, *dominatrix* kind of way." The word "dominatrix" will barely pass through her crimson lips. It will be breathed out so low that the two Correction Services officers conducting the interview will have to lean forward. When the boy came strutting through the door—Debbie forges on with her story—she was still unprepared, and simply blurted out, "You're fired." His radiant emerald eyes "had glared and saddened infinitely." And he was gone. She will swear that she checked his documents and they were in order. Drying a tear from the corner of her eye, she will insist that the contents of her business log and the identity of her clientele are as sacred as the names kept by a priest or a psychopath (by which she means "psychologist," and this will be duly amended in the final record). As to the boy being underage, it will be hard to wring out from Debbie who alerted her about this fact. "Was it one of your homosexual *johns*?" one of the officers will inquire in a knock-off *NYPD Blue*-intonation. Debbie will freeze for a second — (never let them see you sweat). "It must have been one of our clients. He's blond, young, discreet, and always wears a red ski jacket." She will pause to place a Cool Mint Listerine on her small tongue. "How was I to know he was lying about his age? The kid was well recommended by this old acquaintance of mine, a patron of the arts." Then the Correction Officers, much to Debbie's chagrin, will urge her to tell about the first time Bruce, their colleague, showed up at her door.

"Wait please, listen, I think I can help you with what you're looking for." Debbie's former social worker persona kicks in before the hulking male figure hurries out the door. Nanette, the bronzed girl with a Blondissima mane checks him out from over the pages of a recent *Vogue* as she sits on the white leather sofa in the reception area, her fleshy tongue sweeping her upper teeth to erase any trace of lipstick.

Debbie cajoles, "I think we *do* render the most appropriate services for you. Let me show you our lovely portfolio." Bruce walks back in and sits ramrod straight on a rattan armchair across from Nanette. Debbie gives Nanette the unmistakable "get lost" signal, which also stands for "change of guard," and the curvaceous, petite blonde teeters on her stilettos down the narrow corridor in search of one of the male masseurs. Bruce is nervous and stiff; he checks himself in a beveled mirror across the room to make sure his tell-tale crew cut — a dead giveaway — is a bit teased up. Debbie returns with "the portfolio" and a chilled glass of Aqua Libra.

The "Jungle Room" at Paris Place is a small self-contained hell, and the Jacuzzi elevates the temperature into the upper 90s. Bruce examines the palm-tree-patterned cheap duvet cover, sniffs the towels, and begins to neatly undress; he folds the pants over the back of the chair and places his polished shoes straight under the chair. Then he sighs, trying to make up his mind. He hesitantly switches the overhead lights off, leaving a dim side table light enveloping him in a yellowish haze. Five minutes earlier Debbie had crooned, "Interesting request. We successfully cater to gentlemen with wild imaginings, and you will enjoy the 'Jungle Room' in the dark as much as in the light. Pay attention to the realistic soundtrack with streaming brooks and parrots. I love the little shrieks they give, don't you?" For a moment, she batted her eyelashes, and she seemed to hesitate as well.

In his Discharge Report, Bruce will report that he never turned on the light in the Jungle Room and that he never imagined that his behavior there could affect his work performance in any way. At first, he will emphatically deny having any knowledge of Paris Place being also for "gentlemen of a different persuasion," but he will be advised against this absurd phrasing and feeble claim to ignorance. As to his knowledge of the goings on in the apartment upstairs, he will write, "It was a nuisance. I tried unsuccessfully to relocate, but I was swamped with work, and it was difficult to find the time to look for another place. Besides, the vacancy rate that winter was negligible." In closing, Bruce will summarize a couple of prickly incidents between feuding neighbors; one verbal disagreement with his co-worker Connie Manley (they will have been caught by a supervisor when he walks in on them); the failure to sell his apartment "due to mildew accumulation in the bathroom and a host of minor disrepairs"; and the resulting "enormous anxiety and disorientation" in his life. He will also make one passing mention to having taken skiing lessons in Whistler that winter.

Back home from his last day at Correctional Services, several months after the leak from the upstairs bathroom had appeared, with one exact gesture, a blue tie briskly uncoils from under Bruce's crisp blue shirt collar. He unbuttons the shirt, one by one, and disrobes to reveal to the large bare window his solid chest wrapped in a skintight CK microfiber white tank top. After a second thought, he draws the blinds, quickly, with a sure, brawny hand; the evening is winding down out there. It is springtime, but dark clouds have buried the sky. He slips out of his blue pants and carefully folds them over and hangs them on the cedar valet to keep them wrinkle-free. On the sparkling clean kitchen countertop sits Ross and Connie's pristine wedding invitation, open in a perfect solitary display. Ross' voice also fills the answering machine with hesitations and half sentences; some of them about "honeymoon in Vegas" and "homemaking," as if quoted from a bridal catalog. Bruce reaches into the refrigerator for a cold bottle of Mountain Dew, unscrews the cap, and knocks it back.

Bruce's well-aimed finger presses PLAY, and a silver disc spins out the torrent of violin chords released under the torture of Ashley MacIsaac's fingers. Bare and luminous, standing in the center of his room, Bruce cries a tear or two, and spanks the monkey, rough, hard, full of frustration. After a while, he checks the 1950s Bakelite clock in the kitchen and at 8:00 p.m. sharp enters the bathroom and runs hot scalding water in the bathtub, and fixes two bare metal clamps onto his nipples that bite hungrily into the darkened flesh around them. In the middle of a rain forest, barely touched by sunlight, surrounded with steam and violin shrieks, Bruce kneels as a pair of feline emerald eyes materializes out of the golden haze. At the door, a rhinoceros shape also awaits its turn. Bruce tastes all the bitter rain as it pours down his throat, not missing a drop, not a single drop. Once the rain subsides, the feline figure recedes into the darkness, and Bruce calmly turns around, and kneels on the wet tiled floor, in absolute acquiescence. Both visitors withdraw for the day. Maybe tomorrow they will come down the mountain again.

**FASHION VICTIMS**

The drug trade in the Downtown East Side of Vancouver has a new crop of young entrepreneurs. These young men are mainly from Honduras brought here to run the street end of the drug commerce in this devastated neighbourhood. Community workers from the area agree that this migration accelerated when Hurricane Mitch hit Tegucigalpa and other Honduran towns. The hurricane destroyed everything from civic infrastructure to some infamous sweatshops where the fancy Kathy Lee Gifford garments, the brassy morning TV host, were manufactured. In Vancouver, young Hondurans have a background in either *maquiladora* style production or heroin chic exploitation. They are true 'fashion victims'.
*The East Sider Community Newspaper*,
Vancouver, British Columbia

At dusk, Simón paces up and down, passes by the pizza joint where haggard hookers looking like *Vogue* models and working boys, numbed by the -10C°, take a break away from their corners. Been there, done that. He clears his throat and spits thick. A distended vein in his forehead betrays strained thoughts. He walks by the place where he cut his first deal, coke, later, speed. He cases the joint and moves forward. Here is the place where he gutted an old *maricón*, a supernova of blood exploding followed by the squealing of sirens, flashing sequins of reds and blues.

Simón had tried to walk away, as if nothing had happened, as if no one would notice his looks, the bell-bottom jeans sweeping the sidewalks, the fake golden chains, the wiry hair tied tight in a short ponytail, the prominent cheeks and *moreno* skin, and the eyes like dark olives—dead giveaways. For five years, he kept on swaggering as if nothing could faze him, down the corridors, from the remand center to the precinct, from a holding room at an immigration department to a parole officer's cubicle, and from there to a welfare office. Simón made it through the system and came out the other side. On his twenty-second birthday, armed with muscles, clean teeth, cropped hair, and a fierce straight-arrow look, he was again out on the streets of Vancouver. First thing, he called Tegucigalpa, or whatever was left of it—*Mira y veras, mi amorcito, los años ochenta seran mios*—he talked on the phone to his teenage *novia* in Tegucigalpa. They mostly breathed hard through the phone, exchanging few words. Soon his child would be six. He hung up and kissed the little golden cross with the image of *la Señora de Suyapa* suspended from his neck and looked around figuring out how to seize the day. It was February 3.

Outside freezes over. Simón walks by a scuzzy diner where he had worked as a dishwasher and gets an almost comforting whiff of grease. The fat manager has a scar across his left eye to remember not to fuck with Latinos. In exchange, Simón learned that 911 aren't his lucky numbers. He passes the corner where he figured out he was "exotic looking," as an old queen said once. The old homo salivated while stroking a lousy $50 dollar bill from inside his car; bent a finger beckoning Simón to hop in. Around the corner, in the alley, Simón had pounded the shit out of him, spraying saliva and blood all over the fancy dashboard. He had taken his wallet. *¡Maricón, chinga'e'su madre!*

Now, Simón passes the downtown office of the Ministry of Social Services where he was sent to see a social worker after he was released — that was a lucky strike. The social worker turned out to be a fresh-from-school girl, real sweet, squeaky, and earnest. She was so spooked by his intensity that she kept on making quick asides to ease her own tension. She said that she was about his own age when she started working there, a radical lesbian feminist involved in Latin American prorevolutionary causes in town — Simón's silence often elicited more information than what he delivered. Ten minutes later, he had smoothly dragged his client chair closer to her upright case manager seat. Barely speaking ten to twelve words, he had made his way close to her. Smooth. And Simón got pussy-lucky — *¡HmHm! fragancia de papaya fresca* — not a minor feat in the middle of the day and in the very trenches of the enemy. Her irises widened and looked slightly unfocused, like the eyes of an abnegating *virgen* who is tripping the light fantastic. Yet she had stoically kept her composure during the interview. "Address? Work? Next of kin?" she asked. Even when he took his moist fingers away and brought them to his lips and licked them, slowly, as if sucking on the droplets of a ripe fruit, she sat there business-as-usual. At the end of the third interview, she wrote him a check and handed him a form to cash it at the bank. She "strongly suggested" that he do some volunteer work because that could "favorably impress" his parole officer.

His first "assignment" was to volunteer for an AIDS service organization — whatever that was. Simón figured that sick fags would be less anal-retentive than the average *gringo*, and soon he gauged an unforeseen leverage. *Maricones* were instantly drawn to his well-packed arms engraved with cheap tattoos, his piercing gaze under a single eyebrow line, his soccer-player legs, and his silence. The day he walked into the crammed offices, he sent several queens into a tizzy, like sprites in a midsummer dream forest; he wore tight worn-out 501s with a twenty-six-inch waist — one size too small for his 5'5" frame, but large enough to contain the wet dreams of many — and a ragged muscle shirt and the scent of his underarms, which smelled like the traffic outside. Someone later described the sight of Simón and his defiance in the language of ad copy: "dark and robust like a Starbuck's coffee." He was sent to a volunteer coordinator who sent him to visit a young man at the hospital as part of the buddy-program. The coordinator, a motherly, colossal queen with a put-on British accent, explained to Simón that the young man he would visit had been without any visitors and crying for days. He interpreted Simón's enormous silence as interest and began to pontificate while flashing quick nervous glances below Simón's belt.

"This young man is a snotty young queer." The coordinator fired one utterance after the other, sounding like an old typewriter, *clack clack clack*, pausing to breathe and then return the carriage whenever his voice reached a giddy bell-like *ding*. "The virus will move governments and corporations but won't change us one bit. We can barely take care of our dying — fortunately no one is getting old, that would be another concern, wouldn't it? — and much less take care of our young. They probably call that *pedophilia*. How do young men like you learn to be proud?" He didn't wait for an answer that he suspected might not be forthcoming. He caught his breath momentarily and glanced at *it* again — that thing could be growing! He resumed his speech with a florid gesture. "The young get to be queer by chance. Not only that, our young want little to do with gay men. Oh no, they'd rather go for a 'straight-acting, straight-looking' or 'bi' guy" — he marked the quotations with two fingers in the air like little antennas and added in a lower voice — "someone like you..." He cleared his throat and swallowed. He seemed to realize the inappropriateness of his comment and dramatically steered clear of it. "Anyway, this kid—Doug is his name—he has been a runaway, a hustler, and now he has *this*, you know, the virus, poor thing. Let me tell you, I'm seeing it all these days"—he paused to swallow the saliva accumulating between his fangs—"I sure hope *you* are taking care of yourself when you are...er...doing the nasty." He had painstakingly selected the most "down with it" word he could remember from overhearing folks down south during his last holidays. Simón grabbed his cock, shifted it from side to side inside his tight Levi's, shrugged, and left. The coordinator reached for paper tissue to collect the sweat on his forehead.

At St. Paul's, Ward 10 C, Simón found a very slender young man with blond curls shading his even paler forehead; his clear blue eyes were accented by his androgynous grimace. Simón's demeanor became gruffer than usual. His accent thickened round his words. They spoke little or nothing. The sterile scent of disinfectant permeated the slow and awkward visit, and not much would change in the following weeks. Once Doug felt more comfortable, he began to ask small favors. His tentative "Would you get me this?" or "Please, get that" turned into commands—"Get that, will you." Looking away with disdain, Simón said little or nothing as Doug blathered on. Doug paused once in a while to check whether Simón was listening but never looked at him directly. Even when he could take some steps outside of the ward—leaning on Simón's solid arm, head up high like a true princess, holding her IV in the other hand like a sceptre, promenading out onto the roof garden on the fourth floor—he never looked Simón in the eye but kept on talking.

"You know, this is like just bad luck, you know. Like, I'll be fine soon. I'll miss the student doctors. Oh my, they're soo cute—you know what I mean?" The blond stopped and momentarily appraised his short, wiry, dark, and silent escort. "Like, I'm not sure you get it, eh!"

"Yeah, I get it. I get it like you got it, man," spat Simón, "'cause you don't let go, *como perra en celo.*" His words blew up unexpectedly, like an landmine. Doug looked straight into the iron of Simón's eyes, for a instant, and looked away again.

"Thought you didn't speak any English." The boy had been harangued at school not to be a racist, not to invade spaces, and to be polite with foreigners.

"I speak enough to get me what I want."

"How would I know? You don't say much around here."

"*¿Para que molestarse?*" was Simón's retort. "You do all the talkin' anyways."

Before launching into another monologue, the blond declared haughtily, "Well, it's how we, Canadians, communicate. We speak, eh." Doug tossed his pretty head like a young girl and a dizzy spell almost made him loose his footing and his arm got entangled in the IV line and he almost touched the ground. He had to quickly scurry to the nearest bench while hauling his pole heavy with medication bags. Simón only watched.

From that day on, Doug and Simón slowly forged a tense silence, a hostile everyday ritual that was interspersed with clipped words. The few times that Simón said something about himself, he showed profound disdain for the city and its inhabitants. He said that the refugees and the wetbacks, the people he knew, called it the "golden cage" —*es como una mujer bonita pero estupida*, pretty and dull. Sitting and staring out the tenth floor window, sometimes in the morning and sometimes in the afternoon, Simón looked like a passenger in a station, apparently oblivious to Doug's aimless chatter. One day, at the end of March, Simón spat out, "*¡Joder! Guerito, si* *suenas como radio condenado cabrón*—Man! You never stop yakkin'?" He also said that Doug reminded him of his *madre* and his *novia* sitting far away in Tegucigalpa.

"If you ain't sick, man, *te meto la pinga*, so you fuckin' gag'n my big one, *cabrón*, and shut the fuck up."

"You're disgusting. You're—you're high. I should tell the nurses," fired back Doug.

"*Y te quedarias sin macho, maricón*, no one to see you—who'll give a fuck?"

That very same evening, Doug had "an accident" and Simón had to help the overworked nurse clean the young man. Silent tears of rage and indignity trickled down Doug's face, but he was too weakened to get up and clean himself. Once they had finished propping him up, the nurse left, and the evening and the silence fell upon them again.

"*Ya no llores, cabrón*. Shit happens," said Simón and a crooked smile set in Doug's lips. Simón remained unaware of the pun.

"Thank you." Doug's whisper was meek. "Soft touch you got there for such strong hands."

"Can say the same about your *culo*, man, considering...you know—" and Simón shut down for the day.

Gradually, cautiously, they told each other more personal stories. The blond had fled from his family in the province's interior when he had turned sixteen. Simón had crossed borders when he had turned sixteen. He had scratched out a living as a fruit picker, dishwasher, shoplifter, and more, and he had kept on walking, thinking that things could get better up north. He kept on walking as if he had been propelled by Hurricane Mitch and the devastation it had left behind. In the evenings, with the fury of wind and the sight of dust still swirling in his head, Simón would wander through the Downtown East Side a while, chipping some dillies or an eight-ball or whatever, and then go back to his hotel room.

One day, at the end of a long summer, Simón came for his regular visit — Tuesday mornings and Friday afternoons — to find another queen with AIDS in the same bed. A nurse told him the blond kid had not died, he had gone home, his pneumonia was resolved, he was a tad shaky, but he could manage — that was that, no message, and no directions were allowed to be given to visitors, nothing.

"Motherfucker *Canadienses*!" Simón's statement sent the demure nurse fleeing from the room. He left the hospital kicking stones. He never went back there or the AIDS organization.

They ran into each other in an alley, a month or so later, behind Davie Street near the blue garbage bins and the rear entrance to a seedy bathhouse. Doug got spooked and tried to pretend he hadn't seen Simón, but Simón yanked him hard aside by the arm. He was smoking a stinky reefer.

"What the fuck?" Simón gave him a good shake. "*Maricón desgraciado.*"

Doug stuttered, "Hey, long time no see!" with a phony bravado and a mischievous smile. "I sort of. Like, I feel kind of bad about not saying bye, you know. I tell you, it's like, it's totally unlike *me*." They checked each other out like sniffing yard dogs. Simón blew a wad of smoke in his face. The blond had filled out into his normal weight and looked his young age again. He didn't look like many of the other walking dead *maricones* in that part of town. Simón had been working odd jobs as a roofer and a dishwasher, and summer had been generous to his body.

"Fucking ingrateful asshole," blurted Simón and

reclined against the graffiti and half-peeled posters that covered the wall.

"Ungrateful," corrected the other. "There's no need to be rude simply 'cause I didn't give it up for you, honey!" Doug snapped his fingers in the air as he had seen in a music video on TV.

"*No estoy para joder maricones infectados* anyway, ya' sick bitch."

"You wish you could have *this*," the blond's temper was piqued. He perked his ass up.

"Can get me what I want. Only thing you got goin' for you is *un culo rico, marica.*"

"The only brain *you* got going is in your little head, you ignorant..." Doug tried to think quick on his feet. "I give up. You...won't get any of it...you ignorant refugee, you."

"You know this head ain't little." Simón's hand grabbed Doug's and made him cup his thick cock. The blond's face reddened. Simón touched Doug's chin with his fist, slightly, almost tenderly, yet filled with threat.

"Wanna have some?" Simón asked. Doug didn't answer but didn't move his hand either. Simón dragged hard on his joint and, barely placing his lips on Doug's, blew out a long and hard supertoke. Doug inhaled deeply, closing his eyes and keeping his hand on Simón's swelling crotch. Simón pushed him aside and turned to leave.

"Hey," called Doug watching him walk away. "Sorry." Simón didn't turn around.

A month later, one sleepless evening, they bumped into each other again. Simón accepted a beer or two — work was not easy to come by that fall, and he was crashing in a dilapidated downtown hotel. Simón complained bitterly about the phony friendliness and carelessness of West Coasters.

"Aren't you glad you're in Canada, though? It isn't

like the States, eh!"

"No." Single words infused with ire were Simón's staple answers.

"It's not *our* problem you got yourself into a shitload of trouble, eh." The blond tried to push buttons.

"Oh yeah, look who's talking? Eh." He looked at the kid intensely. "*Y lo tuyo maricón, eso es un* whole load of shit."

"Bethcha you'd want to get some of this trouble." Doug's eyes conveyed simmering wanton.

"Yeah. Dream on, bitch." His ample hand traveled like an electrical discharge up Doug's thigh.

"You wish," Doug said, feigning rejection. "Your English is improving."

"Yeah. *Gracias, pero no, gracias.* Don't wanna catch what you got."

They got up to leave, and Doug threw a twenty on the table to cover the drinks. "You wish you could taste what I've got." The blond's innuendo fell flat because Simón's words had bitten him like a rabid Chihuahua, and then Simón punched Doug hard in the stomach.

"*No me hables asi, maricón, o te doy un vergazo de puta madre.* No talkin' to me that way, hear me? Do what Simón says, *¿tu me entiendes?*" Soon after, Simón stepped out and the blond doubled up and vomited and stayed, weeping silently, in the dark corner of the bar.

Still, Doug continued to meet Simón three or four times a week at The Ivanhoe, a seedy out-of-the-way bar on Main and Station, to have a drink, sometimes in silence, sometimes making small talk. The blond took care of the tab and brought him presents—a thick leather belt, a wallet, a white gold ring, a linen shirt—stuff he was shoplifting at the department store where he worked part-time. According to Simón's stern directives, Doug was always to wait for him inside; he would come later. If they met down the street and Simón wasn't alone,

Doug was not to acknowledge him. "Will fuck you up good if you do, bitch. What my *aleros* gonna say?"

Doug, always trying to appease him, steered away from that talk. "Hey. What happened to the chain I gave you last week, Simón?"

Simón slurped his beer, wiped his thick lips, and burped.

"You're wearing a thicker one. You exchanged it or what?"

"Bitch, you like *mi hembra*, man, like the *puta* I was bangin', man. She got it for me. Got rid of the other."

"What did you get for it?" Simón produced some smack-leftovers—skillfully placed some in the long nail of his pinky and placed it under Doug's nose. He vacuumed it up in one snort.

"*Si chupas re'rico, cabrón.*" He stroked the thick gold chain around his neck, hanging dead center in the neck of his his tank top. "Too bad, had to bag the *guerita* bitch—*que me dijo que estaba enculada*—but she can't marry me, 'cause her *chingado trabajo'*n'all."

"You thought you'd marry her? The social worker? What made you think the bitch would marry *you*?"

Simón's hand was coarse and flat against the blond's soft cheek. A trickle of blood leaked down from his right nostril. Doug seemed spooked but sat still. He had been at the end of Simón's short fuse before.

"They are on my fucking case at *la migra, cabrón*, can't go yet, gotta do something." He stopped and looked at Doug. "You think I can marry you?" Doug's eyes widened.

"That legal stuff is in the works, some day it'll happen, but not now," said the kid nursing his reddened face.

"Fuck, you're no good for nothing, *chingado pendejo. Ni para echarse un polvo sirves pues.*"

"We can use a rubber." Doug reached in between Simón's legs with his hands. "I can blow you." Simón raised his hand quickly, and Doug ducked faster and toward Simón's crotch. The bar was quiet, and the old man in the wheelchair at the next table, drunk, kept on bobbing his head, saying nothing, glancing at the pair in the corner.

Simón is crossing the entire neighborhood, taking detours, not going straight, getting drenched and cold, heading in this or that direction. He finally buzzes Doug's apartment; it's late; he is let in and a minute later his strapping figure, backlighted by the light from the hallway, fills the doorframe. His eyes are shadowed as if they are hollow.

"Wow! You? Here? That's a first." Simón does not respond. Doug is wearing nothing, a film of sweat, dripping, covers his body.

"How come you're not wearing a jacket, Simón? It's fucking freezing outside." Although the apartment's heating is on full blast, Doug shivers. "You'll catch a cold. Come in." Without turning the lights on, Doug hops on one leg around the bachelor apartment putting on a pair of boxer shorts. Sitting across from each other on the floor, the blond waits long minutes for Simón to say anything at all. Simón unbuttons his shirt and peels it off.

"Sorry, it's a mess and small—subsidy, you know— what's up?" Simón's hairy chest heaves as he lies back on the floor and fixes his eyes on the ceiling. "You're in deep shit again, right?" The small apartment is bathed in the faint light from the post outside. The rain cries insistently.

"Is it the police? Fuck. You were doing so good."

Simón blurts out, "Why don't you speak Spanish?"

"...What's *this* about?" A pause and Doug snarls, "Why don't *you* fucking speak English?"

"Don't got no fuckin' choice!" Simón leans forward, quickly, almost irate. The sharp mix of alcohol and cigarettes in his breath makes the blond's head crazy. "How come you didn't say?"

"Say what?"

"*Nunca me dijistes que hablas español.*"

Doug shrugged his shoulders. "What does my speaking Spanish got to do with you coming here 'cause you're in trouble?"

"*Te confié* you, bitch." Simón stands and begins to slap him hard back and forth across his face, and then grabs him by the arms. Doug tries to raise his hands to protect his face and retreats. Simón lifts him easily and shakes him hard. "You shoulda trust me too."

"Let fucking go!" Doug reaches for his heated face to find blood and sweat and tears. He realizes not all of it is coming from his lips, some of it is on Simón's hands. It is on his sodden jeans. "Do you have to be so fucking dramatic. Yes, my mother is Mexican, my father is Dutch — fucking fucked up pair they are. Quesnel — that fucking backward shithole town — was hardly the place to speak Spanish, and I was already plenty queer. Was peddling my ass with the hockey team." He pushes Simón away. "Fuck you, Simón. What business is it to you anyway? Where *the fuck* did you find out anyway?"

"Some fag who knows you. I was gonna crash at his place. He told me." They sat back down. "Your father was a sonofabitch, eh!" whispered Simón.

"Couch-surfing eh? Hustling for cash, weren't you?"

"Yeah, the *chingado* asshole wanted some exotic ass, but I was late. You had been there, bitch, givin' it to him." His accent turned to mockery. "*Queria coger* anyway and you told him some *telenovela* about being half Latin, some shit or other — fucked your ass good, eh?"

The blond is livid and tries to slap Simón back, but his hand is firmly intercepted midway. "Fuck you, Simón. I did it for you. You said you needed money. You wanna know: yes, he fucked me. He fucked me good, and I got juiced. It's more than I've ever got from you."

"You got Latino blood still." Simón smiles in the semidarkness and stands up again, not letting go of Doug's hand, and lands a couple of bruising punches on his shoulder. The blond shrieks and recoils onto the floor at Simón's feet, his hand still in Simón's. "Ashamed?" Simón twists Doug's arm back. Doug looks down and begs, but Simón doesn't let go. Simón sneers, "You ashamed? *¿Te averguenza ser latino y ser maricón?* You think you're CBC, eh? Canadian-born Canadian."

"Well, I am."

"*¿Y no te da pena por tu madre, culero desgraciado?*" Simón kicks Doug's ribs and sends him flailing against the wall.

"Fuck no. My mother behaved like a fucking maid and is nothing but a silent alcoholic—dogs are better company that she is." Doug pants reaching for air. "My father is a fucking Christian freak who couldn't wait to fuck me every night. She knew and did fuck all." He grimaces and bends over, then he raises his head and looks up to Simón. "What the fuck is it with you anyway? Are you a fucking family therapist? I seen enough of those motherfuckers."

Simón kneels down and silences him with a long kiss.

"Enough mind-fucking. I've had it," Doug resists. "Go find yourself a bitch to help you, or give you cash, or whatever without...putting out. Someone you can fucking *trust*, if that's what you need so fucking much."

"I thought friends can't fuck."

"Never heard of fuck buddies?"

"*Gringo* shit! Gringos are pigs." Simón stands up. He goes to the bathroom, turns the fluorescent light on, and takes a piss, slightly bowlegged. He comes back, digs into his jeans, and gets a wad of cash and a little bag of coke. They take a fix. Doug flexes his head, leaning back on his arms, exposing his long neck, his long torso, where the sweat pours as if they were standing in the hot sun. Simón bites hard on his nipple, chews his neck, and kisses him again, grabbing on tight to his mane of curls.

"Maybe it's true what they say about Hispanics, eh! Lots of rhythm but small cocks." Doug's tone is now playful.

"*Gringos* got skill, no passion."

"I wanted to tell you things *en tu propia lengua*." The word *lengua* makes him salivate. "I've been listening to Spanish lessons. It's fucking sucky, but I do it anyways." Doug's arms embrace Simón around his narrow waist.

"My tongue is yours—*Mi lengua es tu lengua*," and his face beams. "*Catracho lindo*." Simón is momentarily surprised and smiles, wide and open. They fall, embracing on the crumpled sheets of the futon. Doug shivers, but he is not cold. "I felt so fucking jealous every time you told me you had scored with this or that woman. The only thing I can ask is friendship. You said so. You said I'm better off as your friend, not one of your bitches." Simón remains inscrutable. "I accepted being a small part of your world, Simón, not your buddy, *tu hembra, la familia*, not your enemy, or a social worker, or the parole officer—just me." Tears drip down Doug's face and collect in the bittersweet arc of his smile. "And then there is the doctors. I never know what's gonna happen. All those demented queens parading down the street, the guys who used to fuck me and now avoid me, the ones who are still the same weight that I was, the damned bloodwork..." His voice fades and is drowned out by the desperate trickling of the rainwater against the window pane. "I thought of getting myself a man, any man, to do things for me if I got sick, to clean me up, to hold my hand." Time stands still and transparent.

Simón's warm hands slightly touch Doug's nipples and galvanize his skin. They wrestle, like the ticking hands of a maddened clock, kissing, biting back and forth. Doug buries his head in the messy sheets, smiling and moaning, in pain and joy, pulsating; he crawls the length and width of the apartment, escaping Simón's reach, not trying hard enough, filled inside, carrying Simón's weight and then being carried away while scratching the wood floors with his nails. When they pause, the early garbage collection trucks are beginning to make their sluggish way down the alley. They play with fluids, like children.

"*Eso es lo mio para ti.*"

"*Esto si sabe muy rico papi.*" And Doug's lips miss a viscous drop. They toke again and start over, but this time, unexpectedly, Simón's body glides underneath Doug and swallows him quickly, not giving him time to react, in a hardening silence. The blond closes his eyes as he descends a shaft enveloped in thick steam and the humming of machines, sprockets, gears, pistons, and locks. He is Sigourney Weaver in *Aliens*, his favorite movie. "*Ahorita si seremos aleros, cabrón. Anda, coge fuerte, macho,*" Doug whispers, and though his voice comes out husky, deep inside is a shrill megaphone announcing to a congregation of lonely hearts that his day has come— "You love me, you really, really love me!"

At dawn of the second morning, after a second evening, having never left the apartment or the crystal chemical trance, they pause and look at each other; Ripley looking at the devouring alien. Doug mentally checks his heavy breathing and tells himself this could not be pneumonia again—*no, it's only heavy panting*. They lean against the wall, legs entangled, bathed in the warm bass and treble of music crawling underneath the fuzzy carpet and reverberating through their bodies. The downstairs musician had just got home and is playing acid jazz.

"It was about time, eh! You're such a *macho*. Me, always doing the talking. Sometimes I think I speak in tongues." He looks sternly, "Tsk, tsk, Simón, you say little. I do all the drama."

Simón smiles. "*¿Sabes?* I was jealous." It is an aside.
"Really?"

"*Ya lo oiste.*" Looking away he adds, "That fag told
me you fucked him."

"I've never...fucked a guy before...we needed the
cash, he has lots, you saw his apartment." A cloud
crosses his countenance, and he furrows his brows. "But,
you and me, it's different, good. Very good. A bit out of
hand. You know, no rubbers. I'm positive."

"*Negativo, positivo, la misma mierda.*" Simón's iron
eyes acquire a blue tint in the nascent light of day. "I'm
taking something with me. That's what counts." The acid
jazz has stopped downstairs, and their sweat-drenched
bodies are cooling.

"Taking with you? Where?"

"Gotta go back brother, *esta mierda no da pa'mas aquí.*
Go back to my land."

"My land! Go back to working at a fucking Kathy
Lee Gifford sweatshop?" Doug almost shrieks like a
wounded bird. One blow, like a sudden gust of wind,
comes his way and ruffles his feathers.

"Ouch! Easy on the face, *papi.*"

"That guy, *anoche*, we didn't do anything. I don't
swing *that* way. I just needed some cash."

"I don't get it, Simón." The blond leans forward and
caresses his thick black hair, the lobes of his ears, his
strong nipples, his smooth brown chest, the fat gold
chain. "You Hispanics would never admit to liking ass,
man—what's so wrong with it?"

"*¡Joder!* You're obsessed with ass and juice, *cabrón.*"

"Get real! What else is there?" He pauses. "What else
is there for someone like me?" Doug laughs cynically,
and a sonorous slap lands on his already reddened
cheek. "I'm sorry, Simón, I don't get it...I thought—never
mind. Fuck! You blow hard, baby."

"You like it hard." Simón grabs him sweetly and
draws him close to his chest, so close that Doug can hear

the beating of his heart and the echo of his low voice reverberating through the entire room.

"I needed the cash. I didn't want to ask you again. This *maricón*, I sold him some stuff, he go crazy. Kept on coming on to me. I fucked him. Okay. *Si, lo hice.* But it felt *malo*, like I had promised you me—promised you to be the first. *No lo hicimos* all the way, not like you and me. I got high, *loco, no se*, beat the shit out of him." He pauses to chuckle, a short staccato like hiccups. "*La policia, la migra, que se yo,* they'll be looking for me."

Doug panics. "You can hide here for as long as you want."

"*Yo creo que lo desmadré al marica ese.* Don't get outta this one easy."

Doug does not listen to Simón's forewarning. "We can save money and go away. Maybe even go south together, we can—"

Simón places two fingers in his mouth and with the other hand dips into the leftover smack in a little mirror by the bed and holds it in between his two fingers and reaches down. Doug lifts and lets him in and soon they feel playful again.

"Now do what Simón says."

"*Te quiero mucho Simón.*"

# HOCKEY NIGHT IN CANADA

*"The trouble with a secret life is that it is very frequently a secret from the person who lives it and not at all a secret for the people he encounters."*
— *James Baldwin*, Another Country

I like Vancouver because of its winter and the slow evenings that seep into night. I love the mossy gutters that collect the interminable tears of the season. In the winter I can shelter from public view, cocooned, mesmerized by the litany of raindrops. In the winter, I dream. I go surfing through the channels, sometimes stopping in the soothing pools of blue screen. *Click, click, drop, drop, click.* I used to watch the soaps, but now I prefer to watch hockey games and — my personal favorite — sports news and the interviews with the hockey players. I relish those delicious square heads on the six o'clock news, trampling through a humid locker room, stocky and barrel-chested, sweating buckets. When the camera zooms in for a violent close-up, I can almost taste the salt dripping down the sideburns and through the evening beard stubble. Athletes, artists, and politicians talk game without making any sense at all — who cares? Their features transfix me, these strong mouthpieces that insolently articulate technical nonsense. Inspired by their flickering images, I relieve myself. I see Mark Messier step out of the shower stalls, wearing only a towel around the striking column of his body; he brings back memories — *ah, those French Canadians*. You know what they say about Messier — it's not all urban legend.

A hockey star comes into town incognito, a red-haired stud with a jawline strong as a truck bumper and shoulders broad enough to reach from British Columbia to the Maritimes if he'd lain down across the country. *Ad mare jusque ad mare.* He plays hard, spitting blood — fuck you, asshole, you goof, I'll hurt ya, man, I'll fucking hurt ya — curving his thick lips, spits again, ramming ahead like a locomotive, bodychecking. But today, he's not on the ice. He's taken off, unsupervised, and speeds away fast to Vancouver. No practice, no retreat, and no interviews. Nobody really knows he's headed this way. He steps on the gas. When he crosses the border, the custom officer gushes over him and perks up her tits but cannot see whether he's noticing her behind the mirrored glasses. He doesn't have to take them off; he's no terrorist. Anyway, 9/11 is a distant memory; everybody's into the Stanley Cup finals between rival neighboring countries.

Evening starts to set by the time he checks into a cheap downtown hotel — $50 a night, check-out time is 11 a.m. — under a false name. Once he scribbles a signature onto the registration book, his cap pulled down to his thick eyebrows, he stomps up the creaking stairs, shaking the rain off his oversized Gortex jacket and gripping a key. The old woman at the reception desk doesn't give him a second glance — he's one more in the usual hustler-pimp-pusher rotation. Once in the room, he pulls down the yellowish blind, turns on the pathetic naked bulb, locks the chain on the door, sniffs the moldy air, hides the passport and cash under the cranky mattress, then goes and takes a big spit into the bathroom sink. He disrobes for a scalding shower, barely able to reach the soap with every bit of his sizable humanity under the sluggish drizzle. Back in the room, sitting on the grimy bed cover of faded roses, he lights up a cigarette, coughs, and after a couple of drags puts it out in a stained metal ashtray, turns on the TV, and pops a beer can open. On the eleven o'clock news, he watches his own bragging about an upcoming finals back east and some uninteresting news: wars, hurricanes, budget cutbacks. He picks up the phone to order take-out chow mein. The high-pitched staccato voice confirming the order irritates him. Like a caged animal, he paces the room with heavy strides as he waits for the delivery. He sits again on the end of the bed and turns on some adult pay-per-view movie but soon loses interest—his nine inches anxiously arrested at seven and a half, and not fully at ease. He checks a local newspaper looking for a hooker, someone with an exotic accent and skin color, even a tan will do. His perusal is interrupted by a knock at the door, the delivery guy. He pays him, slams the door, casually throws the chop sticks out the window— *fuck 'em*—and grips a plastic fork to chomp through his double serving of chow mein and spring rolls and washes it down with beer. He burps loudly and chucks the can and the leftovers into the trash can.

I don't get out much. My health hasn't been that good, and I find it boring. Still, after years of living in Vancouver, I think the gay bars are unfriendly and racist—call me sour grapes. I choose a small, seedy, dark bar far from the West End, a dive frequented by the welfare types. I can't stand the posing and smugness of beauty queens in trendy places, the poor service, and the "gay tax." I order a glass of soda water—no ice please, no untreated water—I can't drink alcohol. Fuck it. I can't smoke; I can't eat greasy food. I sit in the far corner of the bar to watch ragged hustlers play pool while courted by old queens whose trembling tentacles hand out money, cigarettes, drinks, and phony compliments, all in an attempt to steal the odd kiss. I too appreciate their damaged beauty, their troubled youth swelling in their tight jeans, overflowing their sleeveless plaid shirts. I too get at once scared and aroused by their callous smirks, their growling stomachs, and their sure billiard shots.

It's a good thing I won't have to be sitting here until the end of my fucking days to see how it all decays—there's something to be said about dying young in the '80s.

The rain outside is cruel and unrelenting. It's getting really late, and I'm waiting for it to subside so I can make the long walk home without getting soaked. A burly man on the opposite side of the bar catches my eye. He's sat there for quite a while, sullen, with a cap too close to his eyebrows, wrapping a blunt hand around a thick mug of dark beer. Only once has he glanced around with those uncanny eyes. The poor lighting, the thick cloud of smoke suspended in midair, and the muffled disco music add a cheap intimacy to this joint—we are the few remaining patrons and the last call is announced. Half an hour later, the waiter comes around to unceremoniously withdraw our drinks so we'll leave. I get up from my stool, hoping the rain has stopped its intense beating. The big man sitting on the other side of the bar momentarily takes his cap off to shake it, gulps the dregs of his last beer, burps as he stands, and turns around, stumbles, bobs his head like a child, and falls heavily to his knees.

I rush to hold him up before keeling over myself, only to be steamrolled under his generous weight. His vomit splatters my only pair of good shoes. The bartender, a fussy queen who thinks this is the fucking Hyatt, frowns, smacks his lips, refuses to help, and runs to fetch a mop to fastidiously smear around the vomit. Disdainfully, he tells me to get "my friend" out of there. *What!* (I'm sitting on the fucking floor, dirty and stunned.) *Whose friend? She* ain't listening to me, *Miss Thing*; she's too busy making a fucking mess around me. The red-haired one begins to mumble incoherencies as the manager comes over to help me haul him out the door. Why bother to explain. We're already dragging our heavy load across the room and out the front door.

Outside the downpour hasn't yielded one bit. I flap my arms like a deranged hen for five minutes; I manage to hail a cab and literally shove Red Hair into the back seat. His cap has fallen off, and I throw it onto his muddy lap. I tuck the heavy coat inside the car and slam the door shut. When the driver asks me for directions, I don't know what to tell him. I try to get away; I simply walk away; but the taxi driver will have none of that and inches forward, tracing my footsteps, rolls down the window, and yells at me in a broken accent that he is either getting an address from me or kicking his big white ass out of his cab. I'm drenched and tired. I shrug, I hesitate, I'm annoyed, and at last I give the driver my address on the East Side and hop in the front seat, digging in my wet pockets to gather the remaining change I have to pay for a fucking taxi ride I didn't intend to take in the first fucking place— *¡Chinga de su madre!*

We get to my stingy place—can't afford much on welfare and Medicare. *El pinche gringo* is not asleep but as good as dead in the back seat. Only when I offer the edgy driver a tip does he help me tug the massive body to my apartment door—luckily on the first floor—with obvious disgust at either the sight of us or the thought of the two of us—a thought that hadn't crossed my mind until I see it flicker in the dark eyes of the taxi driver. The driver drops the guy on me as soon as he gets his tip, and as he turns around he mumbles something nasty about motherfucking queers—you motherfucker Paki, I yell after him *¡me cago en tu turbante, hijo de puta!* I close the door. *What do I do now?* The Viking has been unceremoniously dumped on the floor by my door, barely inside. I curse my fate as I drag him a bit farther into the place. I hope he's not going to die here, for fuck's sake; I came to die in this hole, no place for two. What would I say to the paramedics, to my landlady, Mrs. Frown-

Upon-Every-Fucking-Thing upstairs? Well—fuck me!—didn't I miss having a man so much since no one wants to touch me? Now, I've got a man in my apartment, a huge one at that, and he's impaired, if not dying. Leave it to men to go fucking missing in action.

I'm the one who needs to be nursed, I suffer, I am dying here—but oh no, I gotta attend to this guy's needs. This always gets me into trouble. In my ten years here, I've been misled, beaten up, given the clap and the plague. Here we go again. I hold his head over the shit can to spill out whatever is left of his guts—acidic, pungent. I remove his leather jacket, and in the same painstaking breath, I peel his shirt—*wow...not bad—if only he wasn't so wasted*. I prop him up against the bathroom wall and feel a bout of nausea coming over me. I shouldn't have drunk; mixing booze and meds fucks me up. I'm just about ready to reach over the toilet and puke *my* guts out—this isn't pretty. In ten minutes, I'm passed out right next to him, leaning against his massive chest, and drawling bitterly about who will go first. Who the fuck is my last companion on my last day on earth?

I wake up, my face buried in his crotch. His jeans are wet...or he has pissed them. No one is dead. I'm exhausted. I go out for fun and end up taking care of some big white guy. The paramedics won't be necessary, I decide. He's breathing okay, although it smells like a sewer. His chest heaves like a mountain. His eyes are wide open, bewildered, wild! I'm startled. Fuck, that's all I need now, some sort of psycho or a fucking gay-basher—haven't I lived long enough to learn my lesson? I'm about to jump to my feet and flee when he begins to babble a few words that soon build into a monotonous stream. Are you Hispanic? No, I'm Latino—don't they tell them all the politically correct lingo? Not to this one—*Andale, andale. Si señor. Una cerveza por favor*—he mutters the usual shit. Why not put the *cerveza* up his drunk ass? Mechanically, I prepare some thick coffee. It isn't right for my stomach, but I need clarity. He follows me like a Great Dane, all the while he's muttering and clearing his hoarse throat. We perch unsteadily on my two chairs, pulled up to the only small table I own, and sip the nasty syrup I've brewed. He looks younger now, more together, but not a lot. He still babbles a bit before switching into full confessional mode—don't I know it! I was an altar boy for almost a decade back in Santa Ana. That's how I learned to suck good. He lists the major landmarks of his twenty-some years of life, kind of pathetic, but with a clear tone of arrogance: I done this, I done that, I got this, I got that, I'm a big deal, blah, blah, blah. I'm captivated because he's taken off his damp jeans so casually and now sits in his tight underwear right before my eyes, eyes that have seen no *macho* in a while— ¡Una vision celestial-Milagro de Dios! It's easier to vomit in front of strangers. It's easier to tell an utter stranger everything. There's something therapeutic about it; that's why homos have sex in the dark. Anonymity is a good thing. Then he begins with that shit about "not really intending to be there," at that bar, being sort of lost—heard that broken record, *girlfriend*— the repressed *gringo* shit: unable to get laid when sober, and having to booze it up 'til last call before stumbling down to a park or the tubs, fucked up on something. He pompously attempts to pronounce his name, slurring an inebriated *s*, a name I don't recognize from shit. He pronounces it slooooowly so I can understand; it's not my first language, you see; he pronounces it with the arrogance of those who help the crippled. I ask him one, *one* lousy question, and he launches into an epic psychological riff about seeing men, you know, *seeing* them...but living *normal*—Normal! Fuck that shit. An hour later, he's fast asleep next to my bed having voided all revelations and belches. I lie next to him and fall soundly asleep, thinking that with my luck I'll probably get crabs. My last thought before I doze off: *I should have hidden the knives in the kitchen.*

His buddies have been looking for him, two of them, one big white smooth Polish boy and one hairy Irish one. They come to my door. Alarmed and hungover, I open it, and they come in as if they were the police in my old country searching for drugs. I stand back in fear, but as soon as they see their fellow buddy there, sleeping it off, they calm down. One of them closes the door behind me and begins to ask me questions, lots of questions, while he takes his jacket off. The other shakes his buddy by the shoulder and urges him to leave. Oh, no, they're not asking *him* any questions. Instead they tease *me*. Their buddy is semi-awake and with a raging hard-on; the others laugh and tell him to get his shit together so they can split. The Polish one asks me where the bathroom is. I point it out to him, but instead he approaches me, grabs me brutally by the hair—whatever is left after the chemotherapy—and yanks me down to my knees, takes it out—huge!—and forces me down on him. No time to react, and he is juicing me real good. One thing leads to another, and soon the three of them make me suck them, taking turns taking me from behind. They know what they're doing. It hurts, but I like it. They squirt their juice up my hole; they root for each other as if they were working out at a gym. They play hard.

The daylight jabs my corneas. I wake up. It stings. I throb. The red-haired giant is placidly sleeping next to me. He groans and nearly suffocates me with one bicep casually strewn over my throat. His breaths fouls my face like a hurricane. I get a wild headache. I look at him. Yeah, I've seen a guy who looks like this one on TV—no big deal. I see guys like him in every fucking porn video: smooth, plucked, a wiry, nasty dick that never gives. It takes a whole can of lube and a small case of carpal tunnel syndrome to get them off. When they do get off, they get off with a single groan—*gringos* are so often long on technique, short on words. Fartface—don't know his name—lies in my bed until midday. What if his family and the police are looking for him and accuse me of kidnapping him? Now, he snores; the champion snoozes on my '70s shag carpet of faded green laurels. I let him sleep.

By the time he wakes up, I've watched TV for hours. I'm starving, but there isn't much to eat in my fridge. I've caught up with the news though—never watch the fucking news. Who needs such downers? But, today, the news has been very educational, as they say. When he finally wakes up, I'm watching the Sunday afternoon cooking shows. He shakes his head several times and one wild curl of red hair falls down over his left eye like a flame. He squints and a gesture of pain takes over his grimace. He looks like an adolescent. I hand him two extra-strength Tylenols for his hangover and a box of tissue paper. He doesn't look me in the eye. *Isn't it a bit late for shyness, buddy?* He groggily stands up, roughly 5'9," and drops the blanket—*wow, that's some body you got there*, papi—and disappears into the bathroom where I hear a potent drizzle, several burps and farts. I turn up the volume. He stretches and moans. I turn down the volume a notch. Minutes later he comes out stark naked. While he chows down on the last of my Wonder Bread and I Can't Believe It's Not Butter, we sit there uncomfortably, not saying much. I watch Martha Stewart come up with something fabulous out of nothing at all; he seems lost and mesmerized. He asks me about his clothes. I tell him I put them in the washing machine and dryer downstairs. I'll go and check in ten minutes or so. I ask him whether he needs to use the phone; he says no. I meekly tell him that I took the money out of his jeans before putting it through the washing, and that I took some of what he owed me for the ride last night, and then I tell him how to return downtown in a cab. He mutters "thank you" and the arc of his mouth seems to trace an imperceptible smile — I think it does. I gain courage — don't always know when to shut up — and give him a piece of my mind about drinking to get fucked, repressed *gringos*, homophobia, and being *in the closet*. I don't look at him, my eyes glued to the screen. By way of response, he blurts out something like, "You wish, buddy. You're seriously tripping. I was there by mistake..." — here he huffs — "I don't swing that way. Get me my clothes, will ya? I'm hitting the road." His hard tone is back to what might be his normal testosterone level — aggressive young buck. *Not so fast, papi.* I pick up the clicker, turn off the TV, turn the VCR on, and play him a tape. A recorded segment of the six o'clock news, a sports segment, that announces the upcoming national finals of the junior league or something like that, and shows his pretty face on camera. Miss Red Hair is *on* it. *I'm onto* you, *Miss Thing.*

If experience amounts to anything, I should keep my composure. Quickly, I swap the revealing news tape with one of my fave porn flicks — his face chills. He keeps sitting on the chair, naked, but after a couple of minutes his cock hardens, slowly, and slowly he leans forward to mutter between clenched teeth, "Fuckin' fag, get me my clothes, or I'll fucking break your fucking arms." A tremor shakes me all over, don't know how long it lasts, 6.5 on the Richter scale, the epicenter is in my faint heart. (An earthquake has been overdue in Vancouver for twenty years, scientists say.) I lean forward from the bed, livid, scared shitless, and carefully retort, "Oh, yeah? Well, you do that. But unless you kill me, I'll fuck your life up good. Won't be famous for your hockey game after that — get it?" All of him, which is a lot of humanity, has gone limp. I add, "Now you'd better get yourself together there, Bamm-Bamm, 'cause you're gonna rock my world, and score some game here." He forces a grin that is half-insolent, half-loathing.

Saturday evening is dark, darker than usual; everything is messed up: the lamp by the bed has been knocked over, the pillows are drenched; a sharp smell hangs in the air, and time has paused. I've got a shiner, a black eye that hurts like hell, and my left arm is bruised and strained. On one corner of my bed, sheets torn up, mattress exposed, the red-haired one pants in half-time mode. In fact, he's been able to get the game going; he's played defense. Oddly, I seem to be showing great form, my stick is up, my ass intact. Can I take any more thrashing? The porn tape has rolled to its glorious money-shot end and rewinds automatically. When it fully rewinds, the VCR turns off, and the TV turns on. *Hockey Night in Canada* is on CBC. Score! Unexpectedly, he abandons the idea of killing me slowly by punching me, dismembering me, and twisting my arms — thanks for the short attention span of our youth. Still naked, he leans forward, so far forward his lovely nose almost touches the screen — it has been broken twice, but I learned this later, much later on a TV biography special. He is transported — my mental thanks to the rich charitable queens who handed down their two-year-old VCR to me: *gracias, girls! Will never dish about you again, promise.* I turn it up loud, so loud we can hear the rush of the blades scoring the ice, the sweat, saliva, and blood hitting the boards over the agitated screams of the commentators.

A half-bubble moon pregnant with radiance surfaces in my bed. I approach his moon ass with the greed of a child anticipating an ice cream cone. When I first wade in there, the muscles stiffen and the moist ring recoils; but he does not flinch or turn or move. Inside his bowl, at the core of this steroidal fruit, there is moisture and warmth.

I lap it up. I hesitate but do not withdraw my lips—this is *so* '70s; I can't believe I'm into *this*! The sweet smell and the delicate taste cast away inopportune thoughts of tropical parasites. I am a tourist, and I want to eat at the sidewalk vendor stands. I want to eat raw fish, I want a mouthful from the cracked fruit, I want to ride in fast cars without seat belts again. If they could see me now, those smarmy "I'm clean and safe" queens from the phone lines, the ones who leave skid marks when they get a glance at my lesions. Wait a second, is he turning over? Withdrawing? No, he's moaning a quiet moan as the Canadian team takes a beating, 6-2 from the Americans. This ruffles my fledgling national feathers a bit; it calls for revenge. Open up, open up, leave your net unattended—he does and my serpent tongue, *Quetzalcoatl*, reaches into the deep looking for the seeds of the carnivorous flower, blooming under my kisses and bites. *¡Viva La Malinche! La Malinche* seduced Cortez or was it the other way 'round—who cares? *La Malinche guerrilera, revolucionaria,* now marches on, slowly climbing tongue and cheek, licking, kissing the great slope of his back, the gargantuan spine, climbing each disc to the soft nape of his strong neck—haven't seen many necks in my time, but this one looks good. I bite, and my hands grab onto 100% Grade A rare Texas sirloin steak to make it to the top—I can say that again—the top. I hear the grunts of near victory from the American team; they're giving it to us big time in the third period and one power play; but I come from behind the net to score as I plant my own victorious stick in foreign territory, dark, wet, tight. My hands and my broken limb ache, my head spins, my eyes are swollen and semishut, but the victory is really ours—*thump, thump,* one more pass, and we can win. Sixty seconds and the Canadians are down 7-2, but I am serving my new country, fuck, yeah. Fucking eh! We will, we will rock you! The end of the game finds us all celebrating in a human pile, kissing our teammates, groping under the confusion, drinking spit and sweat, yelling out loud how fucking good the game was.

It's late Sunday night when he stops and turns to face me at the apartment door. He is wearing a red X-large T-shirt that I usually wear to sleep in. (We couldn't find his own shirt. It had been snatched from the laundry room.) His jeans are tighter than they already were last night; now they engrave every inch of his skin. We don't say a word. I don't play the soon-to-be-left wife when he turns and leaves. He halts briefly, takes two steps back, and my inflamed eyes are facing his Chevy-grille-like chest. He leans down and places one slight kiss on my lips. I close the door. I stay inside the apartment with all the lights turned off, the TV off, and quiet tears stream down my face *à la* Maria Felix in *La Mujer de Todos*. A cold scent of full moon takes over the night. I hear the sound of the rain washing away his harsh steps down the street and into the drains. Somehow this idea refreshes my troubled soul. A week later, I will receive a succulent money order in an envelope without a return address. The postmark will read Alberta. An unsigned note will read "*Gracias,*" and I will wonder what for.

<Stick an inch of tongue up your hole>

A pause in cyberspace is a lapse of white noise.

<it's good up there, man!>

His replies are concise, terse almost. Cocktease.

Online, I'm young again, no wrinkles, a full mane of hair, impeccable teeth, and a boner like a liberation obelisk. I have no accent, nothing tints my skin, whiter than white, firm nails, coarse body hair, I'm a Gemini, a double-edged sword, a potent top, "bi-curious"—never "gay," gay is "so out."

<C'mon bud, people send credit card numbers online ALL the time. Send me your email> <It ain't a big deal> A long pause. My writing is stilted. I don't get *the groove*. I used to spraypaint political graffiti when I was young—that was a long time ago, and someplace else, but this is rap of short and "cool" words. Damned kids, brought up on hypertext and thinking in fast-edit mode. They have no memory or guilt, for that matter. I type fast (with three fingers) <Hey ya'll dawg, Spunk, whassup?>

<whassup? You doing the black thang? :)>

I feel like an old man with a bad comb-over.

I knew I was getting older the day I wrote to Spunk <should we rendezvous at the Java cyber café?> in response to *his* response to my personal ad on one of the bareback sites. Rendezvous! He had a field day with that. LOL:) What am I doing flirting with a kid anyway? I don't even like them under thirty. They can't hold their drugs, don't know how to douche, deep-throat, or kiss, and sure as hell don't know how to mix hard-core and a good laugh.

<Spunk is ignoring you or has left the chat room> glares on. Fuck it! Who needs it anyway. I have to correct my students' work. It's Wednesday today, and Ward will be coming by later.

A couple of weeks later I get a phone call at home, a digitized voice.

"Hello, I've talked to you online."

"Me?" I immediately wonder whether this is one of my students speaking in a carefully modulated voice so I can understand — once a foreigner, always a foreigner. Any foreign accent makes them sound out their words like retards.

"Online," he grunts awkwardly.

"Oh...okay, I get it — yeah, of course, how are you? How old are you?" I blurt out. Silence. "Where are you?"

"I'm fine. I'm around." His metallic words are bulleted.

"What's your name? You seem to know mine." I can't help the condescending tone of my voice after years of academic training.

"You call me Spunk." His response is faintly sarcastic.

"Hey, how did you get my phone number?" *Click.* He's off. I press *69 at once. An androgynous mechanical voice says, "The subscriber you are trying to reach does not accept return calls on this number. You will not be charged for this call."

When did we start to migrate from the safe and brutal democracy of the bathhouses to the Ethernet? Never sure of what comes up, what is virtuality or virtuosity. The timing is not all too bad; cruising has become a disembodied activity just as my bones have begun to resent moving too much to find sex. Anyway, it is flattering that Spunk — possibly an old fart passing as a kid — wants to get a hold of me. He keeps chasing me on this site, in the maze of chat rooms. He often changes handles to <tightend> or <gloryhole> but I'm not fooled. He keeps his substance: I can *tell*. We talk casually. He seems interested, and I try to separate facts from fiction.

In the days ahead, I teach, I go to the gym, I eat, I *do* life —
not as exciting as the online playground where Spunk
often lurks ready for a candid conversation — I jack off
twice a day to relieve tension and avoid prostate cancer
(as they say on TV), and I try to cut back on the booze
and weed. Quarterly, I make a call to Montreal to find
out about my son. To do this I have to tolerate his
mother's update of solicitous family "business." Over
the years, my son has only picked up the phone a
handful of times. On those occasions we've talked like
strangers: we stutter, and we pause, too long estranged
to thread a conversation. I have more of a connection
with the eighty students who pack the university
auditorium to dutifully listen to a lecture, even though
most of them have developed the admirable skill of
sleeping with their eyes wide open. I can even carry on
more of a conversation with the man I fuck on
Wednesday evenings or even with the ghostly Spunk
online. I sometimes have good talks with the tricks I turn
at the peep shows on Granville Street on my way back
from campus. I kind of get off on the secret shame and
banality of it all. What would my stiff colleagues say, or
my students for that matter, about my cruising the seedy
peep shows? It wouldn't even be a salacious piece of
gossip. Academics are too conventional to spin good
gossip, especially those in the humanities; we're a bunch
of underpaid and bitter souls. Such petty news would be
simply met by a great deal of silence, the worst
disapproval. They're all busy fucking their graduate
students anyway. Even old whores like me have
standards.

I'm getting curious about Spunk so I log on searching for
him, roaming chat rooms and blind alleys — I feel like I'm
back in the big city I grew up in: a demimonde of
oddballs, gadflies, activists, artists, and closeted
soldiers — the Internet bleaches all personalities, all

motives. Spunk sent a personal profile after I scolded him for having phoned and hanging up. I keep his profile among the posted papers on my bulletin board. It's like a verbal police mug shot: 25, 5'9," 155 lbs., shaved head, smooth skin, black eyes, 8.5 cut, thick, low-hangers, hot bod, piercings, thick tongue, full lips, and an ardent kisser. I added the phrase "ardent kisser." I like it; it seems appropriate. He says he works as a dishwasher, but he will do *more*. Like what? Relocate? Go *back* to school? Back? He says he drives an old motorbike—reminds me of my old Harley before the accident. I collect evidence during our long and arduous jack-off sessions. Spunk does not live in Vancouver—I can tell. He mistakes locations. He's a liar who wants to tell a truth. I, on the other hand, try to remain private. I'm too used to being the teacher—"I *ask* the questions, ladies and gentlemen," I pompously declare to the full auditorium at the beginning of each term. "I *do* accept questions (I take it like a man—I think), but if you are gonna...I mean, if you are *going to* ask me something like 'are you *homosexual*?' you should be ready to answer the same question yourselves. Besides, in my case, the answer to that question would be...duh!" Nobody gets too shocked, interested, or amused by this petty coming-out ritual anymore. I'm considering receding back into the closet to spruce things up.

A week or so after his mysterious phone call, Spunk drops a note in my academic email account. The nerve! This is *not* my Hotmail account. How did he get my university email? It's okay, I tell myself, no one will see it, but on the other hand, they police everything these days. Last term, two wide-eyed first-year sociology girls were reprimanded for downloading kiddie porn—they believed they were doing research.

Mrs. Levitz, the octogenarian who lives across the road, was here last Wednesday to complain demurely about Ward's squeals spilling across the street. She said that "some proclivities might not be in keeping with one's coming of age; they are foolish at best, grotesque at worst." I apologized profusely and accepted the homemade cheesecake slice she brought as an offering for quietude. Our society has lost *that* sense of discretion, decency, and self-criticism: I don't use the toilet in front of others; I gossip in hushed tones; I pretend to listen to most speeches my boring colleagues deliver; and I expect to be reciprocated in the same manner in each one of these civilities.

"May I come in?" A young girl with a red mane of hair, barely controlled by two Hello Kitty pins, pops her head in the door. *Shit! Busted daydreaming again during my "office hours."* Quickly, I close the window with Spunk's message on my screen. I didn't get to read his note. I attend to the student. Her name is Beth. I'll read Spunk's note later.

"Later" turned out to be Sunday evening—midterm exams and piles of dreadful essays to read prevented me from checking Spunk's attachment. I turn on the computer; it ploughs along, purring. I've got to have one of my students fiddle around and upgrade it—maybe that new student in my class. She was saying something about being good at computers when she came to introduce herself as one of my new term research assistants—she's in one of my classes, too. No, I'd better not invite students into my house; they gawk at everything, though most *everything* is kept in the basement. (My *decent* Catholic hangover that lasts a lifetime.) Besides, one time, long ago, one of my colleagues insinuated that I was more or less dragging innocent pupils to my lair of corruption and despair— asshole—"well, it may be misunderstood" was how he put it with pursed lips that have never touched cock. He may be right anyway. His repressed midget-dick homosexuality leaves no room for misunderstanding.

I download a week's worth of emails on my home computer. The usual: a batch of faculty meetings, calls to protest this or the other—they think that because I'm an *out* teacher they can count on me for every fucking march or fundraiser. I don't give a fuck about AIDS—done *that*, buried my friends, done my share of committee work, ho hum. Ah! Here it is. Spunk's was an empty message with an executable attachment that I click open on a knee-jerk reaction.

There are only two lines. <Be online tonite> <Will tell you how and where to meet me> <your Spoogedude>. Fuck! "Tonite" meant last Friday, and I can't respond. This crafty guy conceals his email address every time. I save the message anyway (where there is a lust there is a way). Later, I will get a hold of his address; someone *has* to know how to do that. Aha! The solicitous redhead student might know how to.

The phone rings: it's *that* woman again from Montreal. Fuck her timing.

"How is he?" I ask about my son.

"He's going through a phase."

"A *phase*! What phase?" I bite. She huffs.

"I don't know what it could be this time." Her scorn is basic. "My son has gone through far more than juvenile adjustment. I mean, your estrangement, your legal wrangling over visitations, blah, blah, blah..." I tune out (*Oh, cry me a river*).

"The check is in the mail," I state flatly. "Can I talk to him?"

"No."

I hang up and turn around in my ergonomic desk chair to face my screen that now looks like the opening credits of *The Matrix* with numbers and characters cascading down endlessly. I've been infected—again! For the next five minutes, I curse and fret while pushing every button to no avail. I pull out my course list, the confidential records have registration numbers, addresses, and telephone numbers on them. I frantically search for the red-haired girl—I can't remember her name.

The phone rings.

"Hello, professor? Are you okay? This is Beth speaking. Remember me? I was wondering if you need help with your computer?" Her voice is quiet and sweet. I'm speechless; everybody seems to know my business these days.

I try not to sound annoyed. "I do seem to be needing a bit of help," I say apprehensively.

"I know." Her answer is polite and sure.

"How did you know my number?" I mutter.

"You must have received a virus which has automatically picked up every single email in your address book and sent out a blitz of emails under the name 'Sputnik' or 'Spunk' or something." I gasp. Five minutes later she's on her way, and I squirm in my seat while entertaining gloomy visions of the smarmy silence I will encounter on Monday at the faculty meeting. She works for two hours to repair my email program that evening.

I'd no news from Spunk in a week. It was freezing cold when I stepped out onto my porch to pick up the morning paper. A note slipped out. A two-line message printed on eggshell paper: "You weren't online that night like I told you to. Don't FUCK with me. Be at the Cassiar peep shows on Granville at 8:00 tonite." I'm stunned and at the same time relieved that technology has not completely killed the romantic stalker.

I'm speeding. This is ridiculous. How can I cave in to the demands of some computer hacker, possibly a mongrel? I've just careened around the corner of Clark and

Hastings and can't believe myself. Haven't I learned my lessons? How many times have I been given the wrong directions or been stood up at the fleeting altar of the local phone lines. "Yeah, I'll be there in half an hour, wait for me...naked — or in full leather gear." Too many times, I've waited, and no one showed up — too many. But Spunk has me good this time, didn't think he was *here*, closing in on me. Intermittently, fascination and anger sweep over my senses. My students and colleagues have had a field day with the group email message they all received — I screech to a halt. Ah! A parking space. It's after seven, and I don't have to put coins in. Shit! In fact, it's almost eight fucking thirty! Late again: running on Latino time, one of the hardest habits to break. I march to the Cassiar arcade, the seediest in that block, frequented by the homeless and junkies with AIDS out to get a quick fix of sex or drugs and a few games.

The arcade is almost empty, not much action on Sundays; the usual mix of street and school kids will be back tomorrow. The flare of the arcade neon sign Adult Movies illuminates the No Minors Allowed sign underneath. Inside, it smells musty, of stale cigarette butts. I have no quarters, but first I go in to check the long row of decrepit cubicles, one by one, slowly, like the unsuspecting protagonist in a horror flick who is about to get slashed. Nothing. The long line of cubicles is empty. A row of blue-eyed Cyclopses blankly staring at me. I walk out. There is one grossly fat guy playing pinball at the end of a long row, and the crack of his ass shows where his pants are falling down — that can't be my date. Date? Where did I get that notion? I walk to the young attendant and ask him whether he has seen many guys come into the arcade in the last few hours or so. He looks at me like I'm a total loser and shrugs. I change a five into quarters. I go back in. At least, I can get off. The door creaks shut behind me.

*Clank, clank, clank, clank, clank.* Five coins down the slot —
that will buy me enough time. I press the red button and
surf through boring stuff: two Asian women and a
flabby guy loudly plug each other's orifices with rubber
contraptions. What's new about that? *Click.* Contrived
foreplay between a fake L.A. Latino pizza boy and two
West Hollywood types. *Click.* Three phony leather-clad
men, who are too young, buffed, and plucked to be
credible, finger each other's ass. Is this supposed to pass
for S/M? I need plot, scenes, and dialogue. I linger on a
straight guy with an enormous curved erection who is
fucking a sensational brunette, grunting obscenities like
wanting "it," riding "it," and getting banged. Now, *that's*
dialogue.

There is a noise in the adjacent cubicle; I'm startled.
I didn't hear the stranger sneak in. Before I have time to
resume my task at hand, a cock is slipped through the
greasy glory hole — I'd say this one is a nine-incher,
perfectly chiseled, gorged veins, uncut head, and a slit
the size of a left eye. I think *venereal disease*, but manage
to discard the thought and kneel down. I see nothing
more that a mound of hair. It doesn't smell raunchy; it
tastes bittersweet — not a bad sign. I like *gringo*
bittersweet; it's what made me homo in the first place. I
suck with fruition: "Nice and easy," like I tell Ward
when we role-play — I'm getting too old for that — "nice
and easy," like the Clairol ads on television. Yes! I
needed this tonight. I don't often do this myself; I'm
typecast as a "top" in a town of pillow pushers — well,
and bad experiences too, and the medical cocktails have
all made me reluctant for the good old fluids. I
sometimes get urethra infections from getting serviced
just the same — not *all* risks can be avoided. Hmm, hmm,
this is tender and j-u-i-c-y.

The woman in the flick is deep-throating the trucker
too, nice and easy. Four is company! *Clank, clank, clank,
clank, clank.* Five more quarters down the slot, and I jerk

myself. I wonder when *it* — I mean, *he* will shoot. It's the usual competition: boy meets boy, a duel ensues, and the victor is the one who gets the other one off first and walks away with the precious seed. After five minutes, the erection is still a firm nail through the wall, unwavering. I withdraw and whisper "Wanna join me here?" a bit too loudly for my own good. The answer comes in the way of a solid knock on the plywood partition — his forehead? Maybe Spunk is deaf and mute, that would explain the digitized voice on the phone when he called. The cock does not draw back, and I work it more. "Do you want to come?" I should lay off the polite questions — it's silly carnal etiquette. The tattooed trucker onscreen dictates in a hoarse voice: "That's what you want, bitch, eh? Yeah, getting fuckin' banged, yeah," and she responds something along the lines of "Yes, give it to me! It's sooo good!" — *Should I swallow? I haven't done that in ages!* I anticipate the savor of the hot viscous sap gushing down my throat.

I hardly have the chance to react when the sly oozing Anaconda withdraws into its cave. I kneel there for a moment, in the confessional, thinking, *It'll come back, right?* Then, a little rolled-up note is slipped though the glory hole. The small screen goes blank, and the cubicle goes pitch-black. I forgot to feed more coins into the slot. What happened to the couple in the flick? I burst out of the cubicle, doing up my fly and my belt, and check the next door. It's ajar, and there is no one inside. I'm so flustered when I rush out of the arcade, I forget to ask the attendant if he saw him come out or what he looked like. He probably wouldn't have answered anyway. As soon as I'm inside my truck, I turn on the light and unfold the note: "We'll meet soon. Check your email." My tongue licks whatever traces are left around my lips.

The next week is hell. Lots of work: mail comes and goes almost unnoticed, nothing special, and toward the end of the term I have less time to get on the chat line. I casually plan the end of the year, call friends, arrange for visits, buy baked goods, check my weight, have prescriptions filled out, work out sporadically, teach a few good lessons, check on my mother in her retirement home, and watch the crying rain from my window.

*Ding-dong!* The redhead student made the computer work faster, but she also enabled a fucking perky email notification sound. I browse, and I sip coffee: one from Ward, my dutiful fuck-buddy of Wednesday evenings, to thank me for last night and to tell me that he will be somewhere up in the rugged north working next week. He's so brute and predictable, like an ox. It's almost tedious, but we have an understanding. I don't hear my straight contemporaries moaning about their sex lives being tedious as much as I moan about mine. They accept it. We homosexuals do have an edge, but we want more. I wanted a "normal" family and to eat my cake too. All I got was a pregnant aboriginal princess hitting the roof and going berserk on me. It was Winnipeg, for fuck's sake. I was a political refugee at a time people wrote letters, not emails—my shrink must again hear this chapter and verse of my life.

My memories dissolve rapidly when my eyes catch Spunk's message with raging capital letters <that Ward guy. Too FUCKING E Z for u. I WOULDN'T ASK FOR MERCY. I wouldn't cry after 20 blows> How could he know?

Beth, my student was here, working on the computer, when Ward arrived. She finished soon and scurried timidly out the door. Maybe she forgot to lock the door properly—fucking spaced-out youngsters. Ward and I were drinking coffee (which I later used in his enema to jump-start the session). I had forewarned him on the phone: "Wear something normal, for Chrissake, not a skimpy leather number. Uptight? Yes. Take it or leave it." (They love the humiliation.) I foreclosed the subject. "It's about courtesy and discretion—hear me? There might be a student working on my computer when you come here tomorrow." How come he only manages to look like a total pussy fag when he comes on Wednesdays? Such a burly man, it's unbecoming. I scratch my head, trying to figure out possibilities. Anyway, Ward and I moved to the basement (just in time to avoid him telling me about his Ukrainian past). No one could have seen us there. How could Spunk know...?

The phone rings.

"Hello?" The voice on the other side is muffled. "Seen your email yet?" Spunk's words come through quickly but pronounced one by one.

"Aha." I'm trying to collect my thoughts.

"Surprised?" he asks. I don't utter a word. "I know a lot about you...and you want to know more about me, right?"

"Yes." I can't explain why I'm whispering.

"I've seen you teach. You're awesome." I place my lukewarm mug of coffee on the windowsill and scan outside my window in both directions, but the street is deserted and has an otherworldly glare.

"Go online now." He hangs up.

I log on under my <SternDad> handle. There is a long pause. Evening is a popular time slot, and everybody is playing footsie online. I should get a better modem or a cable connection to be there immediately and obliterate time—and do what? Everything today is too immediate, *bang-bang*. No wonder these kids get infected. They have no time to think, too high on video feeding and crystal meth. Not that I don't like that stuff but...

<Say hello to Spunk> Others in the chat room rush like piranhas to say hello to Spunk, lured by his hot description. His <Pvt. only> room is promptly filled with ghostly gentlemen callers.

<These dudes don't get it often eh! Intense!> he "Pvt.s"

me. <There are many things I have not experienced> <There are many things that you know> <You can teach me>

<Spunk, what are really you up to?> I type as fast as I can. He ignores me, closes our private window, goes back into the chat room and talks dirty to another guy. He's making me suffer, sonofabitch! After five long minutes, he "Pvt.s" me again.

<Did you like me?> <At the Arcade?>

<Was it really you?> <Why did you leave?> I'm throwing a hook here. <Maybe you're a watcher> <You can't face me. You're ashamed. Maybe you're hideous>

<Yeah, right. Like I'm the fat booth attendant showing the crack of his ass and you sucked my cock anyway> The thought simultaneously stokes disgust and morbid lust in me. I wait.

<You're hot-looking in tight jeans, a *total* daddy> He couldn't have possibly seen me through that small glory hole. I won't play anymore unless we play hard, won't have any more backseat driving from this punk. I wait. I don't push any buttons, not while he's pushing mine. After a long minute of silence, he calls back.

<U there?> There's a long pause. <You're pissed?> Another pause.

<Explain yourself right NOW>

After a minute he retorts.

<Geez. Didn't mean to hurt your feelings> <Some of you guys are weird. I got to be careful> <I wanted to check you out first>

<EXPLAIN! You fuck! You're bluffing> <this IS your FIRST time> I'm acting on a hunch.

< Hey. Don't get mad at me. You lied too>

<You have been stalking me, you ruined my email program, my computer, you broke into my private home> <and ABOVE ALL, if you didn't like what you saw you wouldn't be online now, would you?> *Touché!* —I hope.

<U lied> <I had to figure U out> During the pause, someone else's request to talk with me pops up on my

screen <Hey daddy dude. You busy?> to which I reply <fuck you>.

    <U want to meet me?>

    <Yes> I lose my sangfroid. I fire back faster than I should. <When? Where?> Spunk's instructions flicker on the screen line by line. <that hotel right above the Arcade. Meet me there this Friday at 10:00 p.m.> <don't say nothing at the reception desk><tell them you're going to room #13> <wear your 501s and your Harley jacket and your regulation military boots, nothing underneath> This someone has been through my wardrobe—the unspeakable sin! With a sudden change of heart I type <Forget it pal, have no time for your mind-fucking games...> But, before I finish, a cryptic <Spunk is ignoring you or has left the chat room > pops up. May my *fucking* soul be deep-fried in hell. I'll be damned if I go on this date. Date?

I'm wearing my frayed tight 501s, no underwear, my tumescent cock trapped in a thick and heavy metal ring, black boots, and my biker jacket on top, nothing underneath. I should be cold, but I sweat instead, the drops collect around my belt and the rubber of my nipples scratches against a sleeveless come-fuck-me plaid shirt. I coil the whip around my waist and fasten it when I step out of my truck. I'm also carrying a knife, and I think I could use it. This whole proposition is spooky, maybe even the meticulous plan of a serial killer or a gay-basher—it's happened to me before, can happen anytime. I should be watching Christmas movies instead of B-movies to go to sleep. Too much coffee.

    A minute later I enter the dingy hotel. I approach a fat guy sitting behind a table—a sorry excuse for a front desk poorly lit by a naked 40-watt bulb in the smoke-stained ceiling. The entire building smells. *Contagion* flashes through my mind. The fat caretaker surfs the tube, hurried footsteps on creaking planks, a panic-stricken scream interrupted, someone is gutted, the gushing of viscous blood in a close-up—suddenly someone joyously asks, "Who wants to be a millionaire?" I ask the fat guy about the guy in Room #13, and in lieu of an answer he hands me a key without averting his eyes from the screen. He looks like the guy in the arcade a few weeks before. Was this the guy I sucked? Yuck! But...a serial killer? Aren't serial killers supposed to be ruggedly handsome?

I slip the key in and turn it—no more *que será, será* for me, Doris. I push open the shrieking door *à la* Janet Leigh in *Psycho* to settle this whodunit once and for all. Inside the room, the lights are out, and the window sheers, torn in places, flutter slightly. A crisp draft breathes in. In the dark, helped by the faint corridor light, I make out the shape of a bed and someone lying on it.

"Come in, close the door," kindly requests a whisper. I close the door (I didn't know I was this obedient). In the damp darkness of the room, I fumble to find the light switch to my right, and when I find it and flip it, nothing happens.

"Enough of this game, pal." I spit it out, unnerved, without moving an inch.

The voice has jumped to my feet very swiftly, and a pair of arms is now entangled around my legs and my waist. "Forgive me," he says quietly. It is a young voice. "I know this is weird. It had to be like this." Although his phrasing is oddly cliché, his tone is sincere. His breathing warms up my crotch, his words ricochet against my instinctive erection.

"Teach me first, then I'll tell you everything you need to know." I try to push him away. One of his hands caresses the knife in my rear pocket and then clasps onto my coiled scourge. The other unbuttons my fly skillfully, quickly, and his lips slither around me with uncanny dexterity. When he pauses, he makes sure that I hold the whip in one hand.

"I beg you...sir...for your discipline."

I hesitate. I think about it and push him hard and away from me.

"You fucking psycho, where do you get off making my fucking life difficult, embarrassing me in front of my colleagues and students. I'd be crazy to have anything to do with you—" I can't think of any epithets at a time like this. "You fucking...psycho." I didn't mean to go this far, but the situation has made me reconsider. "I will not—hear me?—I will not have anything to do with you unless you let me see who you are." After a long moment, he slowly stands up, and breath that smells of me wafts in my face.

"I'm Spunk, you know it." In the chiaroscuro of the room, I can see a chiseled body and traces of an angered expression. "How come you can role-play all that stupid daddy-son bullshit with a forty-year-old? Isn't *that* embarrassing? But you can't deal with the real thing, eh?" With rage, Spunk punctuates every word of the next sentence, "Or-is-it-that-you-don't-really-have-the-guts-to-get-to-know-me?" My body is flushed with adrenaline. I strike hard where the unidentifiable mouth should be, and traces of Spunk's spit hit my knuckles and my face.

He comes at me. Quickly. I react out of panic and discharge another blow to his face that spins him around and makes him topple and crawl over to the bed. I remember my grip on the whip, and I begin to thrash his wide back. His body curls in pain as if pulled by puppet strings. I strike hard again and again until there is nothing but his quiet sobs, and I, exhausted, sit by this coiled shadow on the creaking bed.

I'm on my back. He has ingeniously rolled a condom on me with his mouth. Still sobbing in pain, he lubricates it well, and then like greased lightning, without a warning, he ferociously impales himself and lets out a deep lament. In the subtle moonlight, I can behold his agile figure enveloped in a tight, thick black leather cinch that runs from right under his sturdy nipples to his compact waist. I run my hands down his tense muscles, the soft pelt of his back. While he is straddling me, he places a bottle of poppers under my nose and I...inhale—Do I ever! I haven't done this shit since the '70s—mighty good stuff it is. *Wow!* I'm heaving, shoving into his core, and then I see a nebula formed by a million little stars, like an admirable screen saver! *Wow!* He disengages so fast, grabs something from a chair nearby, and puts it on. Momentarily paralyzed by the poppers, I can't react. He opens and closes the door right away and flees the room. I pulsate like a neon nightingale under a single moonbeam that slips in through the torn sheers. Somewhere far away, in the recesses of my memory, I hear Grace Jones croon that the hunter gets hunted by the game.

All through Christmas and New Year's I could only think of Spunk. I was distracted to the world, didn't send cards, didn't open them. I missed a couple of alarmed calls from Montreal on the answering machine, sent another check, and a present for my son. I bought a present for my mother that she didn't even open, and visited with Mrs. Levitz across the street and sipped tea. I did what we all do—dispensed money in lieu of love. Finally around mid-January, under the guise of <Pup>, Spunk came and found me in a late-night chat room.

    <did you ever wonder if it was really me in the room?>

    <enough mind-fucking, don't you think?><too much of that going on with fags>

    <I'm not a fag>

    <see what I mean?><you fool yourself><but><that's not my issue><you're too young for me>

    <i am not FOR you> <but you want me, right?> <i had to leave but I'm back in town> <i want to be with you again>

Don't know how I got myself this deep, but slowly, like his moonlit figure in the dark room of the dingy hotel downtown, he strings me along like a Scheherazade in the next thousand-and-one emails.

In the cold and drizzly nights of January we met again. Entangled in long embraces, clasped around each other, limbs and sighs melting in the obscurity of Room #13. Spunk said little. He moaned and arched under my weight; he tenderly anointed my feet, my hands, and lips. I sometimes thought that he was a young girl passing for a tough young man, or a gorgeous body with a disfigured face, or an androgynous alien, but when I reached for his cheeks, his mouth, it was all intact, there were no fangs, no protuberances. There was a row of perfect teeth, a fleshy tongue that would come to meet me, and a deep throat that would swallow my tongue and soul and only spit it out when we both couldn't breathe anymore. We would then, before our skin would let us down, chase the dragon together and venture further into the trembling night. In the shivering morning, when he would do his disappearing act and I was left alone, I would feel diluted like the water drops trickling down the rusty rain gutters outside.

Any sensible person would have made an effort to find him out, to unearth his face, to confront him in daylight, but I became so scared of losing him. His sweet face would come last, I thought. Spunk asked shy-but-intriguing questions in husky tones. I learned how to trust him, and I told him much about me: how I had gotten to this city, and where I had lived before. I didn't try to stop him every time he quietly got dressed in the dark and stepped out at the break of the telling light. At the end of February, we met one last time in that hotel. I had decided to ask him to come home with me. I would tie him up, if that was what it took, and kidnap him from this twilight and drag him into the light of day.

Before I can say anything, he places his index finger on my lips, a kiss on my cheek, on my neck. "Soon I'll have to go." My throat dries. And in a hush, he makes a request, "Ride me bareback tonight." It is plainly stated. I try to swallow.

I say, "There's something you should know—" but he interrupts me.

"I know it. It's okay. I'm positive too."

"I have not deceived you. We've played it safe." This is prudish and of such little meaning, but I'm never able to contain the melancholy that invades me when such news is delivered.

"You've said that we always deceive: it's love...you said something like this."

"Yeah, so we've been fooling each other all along, eh?" I can't help the bitter tone in my voice.

Spunk repeats a line I said to him one night, slowly unraveling it from his memory, "You said that a truce in the vastness of one's life is better than nothing."

I'm embarrassed by the pomposity of what I've said and that he recalls it so clearly. I think it's a badly translated line from a foreign poet. "It is a *truce*, all right, a reprieve in a long and tedious battle—something like that." I'm self-conscious. I sound like those somber characters in European movies—I watch them in between porn flicks—in which thin people always turn sex into a languid dialogue about "being."

Spunk is wearing no harness, no chains, no rubber; it's only his flesh against my flesh tonight. "Tie me up," he says as his hand slips a thick rope into mine. It feels slippery, like a lizard. I comply and bind his hands behind his neck and his feet wide apart. Once I'm inside, thrusting, my mind blooms in a thousand iridescent flowers—some are of yellow guilt, some are lust red heat and flames, some are black as a hole in the night. I stop, not horrified, but I stop. I withdraw from inside him and grab him by the hair, stretching his neck so I can catch a sparkle of the outside light in the hollow of his eyes; there are tears streaming down his face. I kiss him for a long, long time. I cry silently, and on a hunch, I call his bluff.

"This is stupid, and you know it. You don't need to prove anything by doing this. You got me as it is. You got me for good, forever. I'll be here if you come back...but if you come back, come back in the light of day."

"I promise, once I have you inside I will reveal myself to you. I promise." His words cast a spell as kind as the impending morning, and I resume my deranged riding of him, away from the darkness of this fateful night. I will give him *my* gift. But, again, I stop. I'm about to blow inside him. His hand restraints have come half-undone. Spunk cries and is begging me to continue riding without thinking, and I want that so much. We have only this second to pause and think.

After that night I've never seen Spunk again. I often aimlessly wander the vastness of the online domains like Lucia di Lammermoor. What used to be an arid land of clicks and beeps has acquired the romantic allure of a mysterious dreamworld where I migrate from East to West, North to South, like a mechanical bride, left at the altar with a bouquet of withering leather whips, talking to strangers, asking them if they've seen the one I love. I check my email with obsessive regularity and a couple of times I believe I have found one or two notes from him, like messages in a bottle, under other names, written in a different tone, less playful, almost compassionate. When spring comes along I'll be drained.

I tried to find Beth, the redhead student who helped me

the year before with my computer, to figure out a way to track down the source code of Spunk's email—she seemed reliable—but she had apparently left school. On my own, I felt almost scared to pursue this cyber-investigation. I see Ward, the man I fuck on Wednesday evenings, absentmindedly, loudly, upstairs, with the windows wide open. If Spunk is still around, he can see me. Unfortunately, Mrs. Levitz can see us too, and she came to complain. Politely, she told me that although she was "quite modern" and had vacationed often in Florida, there were some pastimes that at her age were best left to the imagination. I once more apologized profusely. I'll have to stop beating Ward up, no matter how much he likes it, before we become too much like old gargoyles hanging from chains. In the meantime, I've moved all the equipment again to the basement. Ward was a miner for a long time; he's used to claustrophobic cubicles.

Today spring seems to have taken hold of this place at last. I collect enough energy to return calls, and I follow my list painstakingly. I call Montreal last. It has been almost a month since the mother of my son left a couple of messages.

When I try to apologize, she barks, "Didn't expect any different from you. We went through a difficult phase."

"What is it?" I am intrigued. "What is it?"

"It's okay now. Your son left twice in November and then in January. I didn't want to call the police. He's back, he's fine—it was a phase—of course, *we* talked it out." A chill runs down my spine.

"Where did he go?" I ask flatly. I feel a mix of anger and embarrassment that my offspring is now a runaway. What I teach as theory to my students has come to bite me in the ass.

"He says he was 'around.' In the city, he says, but I

suspect he went away. His girlfriend was studying somewhere else, and she's back too." She hates being legally bound to let me know what our son is up to. I think she only wanted a child to build a cause around: the protection of the innocent from the depraved, the Native single mother impregnated by a handsome fly-by-night—more like a wetback, really, and queer to boot. We've rehearsed all the angry lines before. In the end, I don't understand her maternal instinct. And though I know I'm a good-but-stern "dad" to my "boys," who in their self-righteous mind would ever accept that as fathering?

She continues, "Maybe it was drugs—maybe. You know most Native kids are neglected and fall into the life—anyway, he's okay, says he'll go to college in the fall. He's saving, says he was working in—"

"A video arcade," I mutter.

"How did you know that?!" She sounds surprised. A ghost dances over my grave while I slowly conjure up the image of the handsome attendant at the Cassiar Arcade on Granville Street, the young man who had studied me with deep dark eyes while I was counting the change in quarters, before getting into the cubicles.

The mother of my son is officiously running down a list of quarterly expenses that will be totaled up with a request for a check I'm to mail as soon as possible.

She concludes with a sigh, "Well, he's about to turn nineteen. You won't have to deal with us anymore."

"I want him to go to school. I said I would pay," I insist meekly. Suddenly, something clicks in mind. "What's his girlfriend's name?" My heart races.

"Her name? Beth, I think—anyway, what does that have to do with anything?"

"Never mind. Anything else?"

Unexpectedly, she veers off her usual song and dance. "One day your son will want to meet you, I'm afraid...I can send you a photo." I don't utter a word. "I wish, I mean, for his well-being, after all these years—"

"You wish what?" I whisper.

"That you'll do the right thing and not—he's very mature, but in some ways he might have your...," she pauses. The strange fear that's crept up inside me is now congealing in my veins. "Well, when you were his age, you were—"

I cut her off. I say, "It was a small town, and I was trying too hard."

She starts, "I don't want my son to turn—"

I complete the sentence. "Out like me?"

"I *had* to protect us." Then, her voice lowers and commands, fatefully, almost vengefully. "Don't try and contact him now."

A flashback of police lights, child protection services, and angry voices. My eyes well up with tears.

"Don't send a photo. Never," I say.

I hang up and cry.

# KILLING ME SOFTLY

Finding out how a story ends right at the start often does matter. Adriaan came from Holland. Some years after, he met a fifty-something Chilean exile from the 1973 bloody coup of Augusto Pinochet: Pablo. They had a relationship, until the day that Adriaan decided to break it off and go try a different kind of living in another city and Pablo ruined his life. Maria Elena, Pablo's wife, was privy to some of this and tried to rescue Adriaan. It is impossible to know whether she helped at all. A labyrinth of streets, streetcars, trains, highways, telephone lines, the veins that keep America simultaneously connected and worlds apart, swallowed Adriaan's footsteps.

Where do shooting stars go to exhale their last breath in the firmament of our destiny? No matter how much advance notice we have, the pain of seeing them die won't stop the searing of our hearts. It is better to know in advance that Adriaan's heart was searing at the end of those three long years and before his disappearance; one more character out of a scene of two hundred and fifty million individuals—one more heartbreak that inhales, aches, sighs, and vanishes into thin air. Adriaan's trajectory, the trajectory of a zigzagging satellite in the busy skies, ended with an awkwardly earthbound conversation with Maria Elena, at dusk, in Dolores Park where they had agreed to meet. They sat on one of those hard park benches with the city laid out at their feet, like an innocent-looking-but-insinuating boy in an old oil painting, almost mocking their pain, almost sheltering and inviting but distant. San Francisco, always cajoling and cozy. Adriaan had already begun to live on the streets, and his deep-set blue gray eyes had receded farther into their frames. His skin was stretched like a canvas over his firm bones, withdrawn, but his eyes remained still and limpid. He had some red pockmarks on his face and arms, the signs of tearing at one's own flesh while raging at life.

When they arrived at their meeting place and time, they soon recognized one another, as if they had seen each other before. (She had. Briefly. Furtively.) She sized up his tall bony frame, looking taller at her side, a once-sturdy architecture that seemed to be crumbling under the intermittent, seismic, Tourette-like spasms, the slurring of speech. By virtue of her intuition, Maria Elena could see through Adriaan's strange choreography; she could see past his frayed clothes, unkempt but oddly fashionable, the chic of the destitute, the chic of magazine covers. They sat facing the landscape, not looking at each other, polite but careful. They spoke into the air in front of them, their words muffled by rush-hour traffic; well-turned-out passersby eyed them with vague wonder upon seeing an older and demure Latino woman sitting with a junkie. San Franciscans are bleeding hearts, often intensely aware of the contagion of poverty and disgrace. No one is free from falling.

Adriaan was almost apologetic, sweet, as they both danced in careful circles around the theme of their love for Pablo. Trying hard to approach the other's solitude without hurting—there could not possibly be more hurting—fumbling through the fogginess of this episode in their lives, two ships passing in the night guided by one strange beacon, Pablo, the man whose silver needles continued to puncture through their lives as if pushing and pulling through a narrowed artery. Adriaan was trying with all his might to understand the detour of his life into Pablo's past. They talked little about what had made Pablo react the way he had, confiding in a man, confiding like he had with the very few close friends he had had in the past, not in the U.S., not in this American life. *Pablo became the friend I didn't have*, sighed Adrian. He said he understood their family, their humble but comfortable lives, their teenage son and daughter, their future (they had a future). Adriaan said he understood what in Pablo's life makes him act the way he does. Maria Elena's tears poured quietly down her cheeks, and she collected them from time to time in a handkerchief that she clutched firmly in her left hand. Adriaan had not spoken this much to anyone — no social worker, counselor, or fellow streetwalker — in the last few months. It was important for him to say all these things, to find an understanding, and he had tried hard to be good and clear for this conversation. Maria Elena could help; they could sign an armistice to lay down their invisible weapons. They didn't say anything at times and slipped into a quiet despair. They seemed to be waiting for signals from someone. People in California wait for signals all their lives — from the mothership, the gurus, the activists, and the governors. Both of them had been waiting for signals from Pablo for so long. He remained elusive, cryptic, and mysterious. When Adriaan finished what he could say, Maria Elena's right hand was softly holding his left hand. She turned to him, looked him straight in his blue gray eyes, and said, *Pablo is a monster. You must leave.*

There were many things that no one saw; certainly Maria Elena didn't. But she could guess, and the doubt weighed on her chest at night, weighed on the lumbering of her feet during the day. She could not see, but it was as if she could. Desire knows little privacy because it is revealed in a myriad of everyday gestures. She could have almost seen, maybe by looking up at a window on the fourth floor on Franklin Street, through a dimly lit curtain, how the lukewarm wind blew tenderly, the way someone blows sweet nothings in someone's ear, on a late September night, the way the wind was coming through those curtains of that window left slightly ajar to soothe their loving. That evening Pablo was impressed by the perplexing notion that he was falling for Adriaan. He sought refuge from these confusing thoughts by burying his face in the concave shelter of Adriaan's armpit.

Adriaan had traveled all the way to America to escape his Calvinist family and a boring countryside life that was choking him. Either by searching for the homosexual American dream or by simply being guided by his free spirit, he ended up in this one unreal little enclave where a great number of its male inhabitants happen to be self-exiled homosexual misfits from the bowels of an otherwise belligerent and hostile country. Each year, a flock of youngsters from Middle America and elsewhere, ones who truly believe that one can be a star or a tycoon or a famous serial killer or a significant statistic by simply trying hard enough, migrate to San Francisco. There, they model their bodies after the photos in the magazines and their everyday speech after the advertising copy. It was not that Adriaan was unhappy bathing in the melting pot or that he had not surmised how very different it really was outside San Francisco. It was simply that he was far too judicious for such major generalizations. In his few emails to a good friend he had left behind in the Netherlands, he admitted that the first five of his ten years in the U.S. had been hard. He had done lots of different menial jobs — *way below what I am capable of doing*, he wrote, *but it is a start* — but he was only twenty when he had arrived. What more could an immigrant expect? Even a white, chiseled-chin, six-foot-five, horse-hung one like him. No road or hole is lined with gold. And life by the Bay rewarded him with its ice-dry allure of plentiful sex, plague or no plague, and drugs. Surprisingly, it had taken Adriaan a good six years before he had gotten infected; a reasonable amount given his great appetite for everything, and the ease with which he lived in solitude, driving young and old men crazy, and his bent for highs, tricks, and risks. He worked to have enough free time to bike around the city taking it all in, to go to the beach and to the gym, and to party with strangers.

On Tuesdays and Thursdays, after the delicious meals that Adriaan always put on the small kitchen table before them, Pablo would smoke some strong weed, and they would engage in a polite and gentle ritual. Music played, seasons changed, Adriaan had other men in his bed, but he began to feel different, special, toward Pablo—almost protective. Pablo, slowly, let his guard down, and allowed his stealthy fears and reminiscences to come ashore and pour out from his lips in smiles and handpicked secrets. Pablo would later snuggle up on the one existing futon in Adriaan's tiny apartment, huffing that he was getting old and tired, and as the weed made him high, he would start speaking in tongues of agitated poetic nonsense and enigmatic assertions. He said he had been a psychologist in Chile and was working for a semiunderground cell even two years after the 1973 coup d'état by Pinochet. But they had been betrayed, and some of his colleagues had been "disappeared." His eyes nearly welled up. His family had been threatened, and after quick and fretful planning, and with the help of a church or some agency, they had all been able to escape to Argentina, briefly, and later to the U.S. Pablo was a good father to his teenage children, a provider to his wife, a good-humored and tough worker, and a loyal lover to Adriaan, twice a week, on the days he told his wife he was running the midnight shift at the Lookout, a detox center in the Tenderloin. He had met Adriaan three years earlier at the Lookout.

Adriaan had never been through a detox program, but he had become familiar with them while volunteering briefly as a Hep C– and HIV-outreach worker and later as a fundraiser for some community charity. His doctor had suggested staying away from the drama of drugs on the streets if he wanted to maintain the tight rein he seemed to have on his use: sometimes bingeing, sometimes staying away during periods of intense work and creativity. In general, Adriaan applied to his life and his own habits what from the outside could have been easily perceived as a pragmatic Dutch approach to life (and euthanasia and death), but Pablo, tremendously superstitious as he was, blamed it all on his Taurus ascendant (hence his systematic pace and his pragmatism). In either case, Adriaan had stalwartly approached his budding relationship with Pablo, who was cagey and high-strung at first. After some months went by, the scheduled fuck-buddy drop-ins morphed into a sort of shapeless friendship that had no more commitment than two nights a week, then later... Adriaan had first had sex with Pablo on one of those quick drop-ins, during Pablo's day shift — the night-shift alibi was created later to be able to spend those two nights a week with Adriaan — and he felt a rare interest in Pablo's petty neuroses, his counterfeit confidence, his short stature, and his stubbly beard. Pablo, about twenty years Adriaan's senior, was a man who boasted much about knowing about many things in life, and yet was often obscure about what exactly he did know. *He is intriguing because he is weird* was Adriaan's description to his friend in Holland. What made Pablo mildly attractive to him was that first moment: After they had talked enough — they had agreed on some ludicrous excuse to come to Adriaan's apartment, an excuse that Pablo felt he had to come up with (he was, after all, a "man who has sex with men" — political shorthand for closeted or bisexual) — there was that moment where Pablo dropped a hint of a reminiscence in almost poetic language and his eyes welled up. Notwithstanding, that first visit was a disaster. Pablo accepted a toke, and this calmed him down a bit. But his silences and cautious looks continued. After a while they started talking, and Pablo again became more and more agitated. Adriaan was on the alert at times during that syncopated conversation, mindful of his cellphone and the door. The toke garbled Pablo's words and made his eyes fidgety and let sentences like *I am a responsible head of a family* and *a real man never lets another man disrespect him* escape from his lips. He had paced the room, although Adriaan had told him to try to walk lightly as his downstairs neighbors had complained in the past about the (fucking) noise upstairs. Pablo said, *Probably happens a lot to a guys like you*. Adriaan was pissed and asked him to leave; Pablo said he needed to splash his (flustered) face with cold water. It was then, when he walked into Adriaan's bathroom, that he saw the small 5cc syringe.

Over the course of several encounters, Pablo slowly went from strange to intriguing. He was finally able to loosen his shoulders, open his eyes, stay in the present, and be with Adriaan and...stop talking. It was a month later when Adriaan asked kindly whether Pablo would mind if he took a *hit*. Pablo said he didn't. Adriaan asked whether Pablo would disapprove of his *slamming* it while Pablo was fucking him. *See? The rabid Chihuahua's rear-ending the Great Dane*, Adriaan thought while Pablo was hard at work, with engorged paws and salivating tongue. When the effort verged on overcoming his stamina, Adriaan slipped a rhomboid little blue pill down Pablo's throat with his long index finger and kept it there, gagging, choking until it was accepted. Many hours were spent in the throes of chemistry (followed by a mind-splitting morning headache), but they allowed Pablo to perform feats of daring and indelible tenderness and later to sweetly fall asleep inside the young man. In a few hours, he would be crossing the East Bay to go home.

In those hours they spent together, they were off to another place. A year into their relationship, Pablo took a hit; he snorted it, and the Chihuahua dismounted with a flaccid erection and all the consuming thoughts of the world converging on the whirlpool of his hole. Seeing Pablo turn from Chihuahua into a lap poodle, showing himself, begging for meat, made Adriaan break into laughter. Earlier that night, during one of Adriaan's delicious meals, Pablo had made a big fuss about the lack of hygiene among the junkies at the Lookout. How he often had to take them to task on the universal precautions guidelines; he even had to admonish his co-workers all the time. Now he was licking the sweat drops from Adriaan's hands, the floor, the bathroom floor, rabidly, huffing the odors, going out of control. Adriaan slapped him hard across the face, grabbed his neck, and straddled him with an enlarged spirit. The Great Dane slammed and banged and ploughed and threw a mean fuck. He fucked the light fantastic and ended up with a prodigious and excellent supernova, like the Milky Way darting up and across the black sky and searching for the light coming from Pablo's gaping mouth. Pablo's eyes widened and whirred, setting off a deafening siren in his ears, a siren that could summon all sailors and stevedores from Rotterdam to the South Bay. Pablo's legs caved in, his eyes welled up, his nipples bled, his teeth chattered like swinging shutters in the chill and storm of winter. The walls trembled with sinister delight. Every pulsation was recorded and repeated—like a fairy tale, to himself, to Adriaan, in Pablo's own words, later, much later—and through the following encounter, and the next one, and the next, trying to reach another horizon, farther. It hurt, but there was no stopping. Desire dictated giving in.

In a detox center one has to be unsentimental. Also, one has to be fairly stable, because it is maddening in its monotony of tawdry drama, formulaic scripts, and tedious emergencies. Pablo had started there at minimum wage, but as he managed to earn some counseling and outreach work certifications at night school, he started getting better hours and a better salary. Pablo could stay longer at home, and eventually Maria Elena could work fewer hours and devote more time to her husband and teenagers. They had a modest-but-well-kept house in Oakland, and their children grew into teenagers with minor incidents, some weed-smoking, some trouble, but with a strong sense of pride, and a ghostly notion of a motherland as seen in photographs, a landscape of people and traffic where they would likely never go, a strange planet, a good topic for essays in school.

Adriaan taught Pablo to come in from the street on Tuesdays and Thursdays, to be joyful, to kiss with a mouthful of supple lips, inserting his own long thick fingers between Pablo's rather selfish lips, running his fingertips across his face, his ears, through his salt-and-pepper hair, and pulling him out of his clothes, softly at first, like layers of skin, and then swiftly to ease his discomfort of being exposed. Adriaan taught Pablo to crawl back into his skin, right before a mirror, supporting him from behind, like a good young brother; he made him recognize his old surgical scars, the moles, the orifices, and the shame, and he made him discard them along with his street clothes. Things had changed radically from that first time Pablo came to visit with a stupid excuse, something that had something to do with nothing, maybe it involved the fundraising campaign in which Adriaan was working or volunteering. That first time, they had a coffee and shared a conversation about nothing in particular. In the future, they would have similar conversations about nothing, but they were brimming with a tender desire to understand each other's strange worlds. Pablo would sometimes play old *boleros* from Lucho Gatica on the CD player, and his sentimental crooning would suffuse the air with a kitschy sense of drama that both amused and confused Adriaan.

Things between them soured three years later. They had had a couple of altercations, but Adriaan had kept on receiving Pablo in spite of himself. Adriaan had wanted to get away. He had gotten an offer to cook for a touring dance company, but Pablo, instead of showing support, had clearly discouraged him. He counseled him against a life on the road, the challenges and the health perils. Soon after, one late night, for the first time, Pablo produced a small bag of something as coarse as salt, bitter to the taste buds, and potent. He said that one of his clients at the Lookout had left it behind, that Adriaan should try it, that it would relax him. Adriaan said he preferred to use his own drugs, from a good dealer, from known origins. He was sure what it contained—almost sure, anyway—most of the time. Pablo's tone might have changed to a deeper whir that was strangely seductive as he cajoled and soon after helped himself to Adriaan's rigs and carefully cooked him a dose. He boiled the water, prepared the needle, dissolved one of the small purifying pills provided by the Needle Exchange Program, and mixed the water with the cooked rock. There was something paternal in his talk; there was something vaguely familiar for Adriaan in the newness of some of his actions. He did not try to stop him but watched him intensely. As an alchemist, Pablo seemed so confident. He did not look like an older brother he could fuck sweetly until he cried. Adriaan had told him about his older brother the first time he had fucked Pablo, trying to calm him down, to get him to stop shaking. He had told him about his older brother — what a stupid fantasy, what a cliché — but he bought it wholeheartedly and had eventually stopped his skittishness to rest beneath Adriaan's broad chest and shoulders. There, under his arm and chest, Pablo had waited, eyes wide open like a child, for the young man to fully drape himself over him and protect him from the monsoon of chilled rain that trickled down on their bodies. (He had buried his face in Adriaan's armpit and chest and wept.) Adriaan understood that it was the first time Pablo had been with a man. He had acted with the same care that, three years later, Pablo would take in cooking Adriaan's fix. Pablo, attentively, cleaned Adriaan's arm, draped his hand over Adriaan's to make him clench a fist, surveyed his thick skin, and found a small protruding vein in the branches along his robust arm. *I have never let someone do this for me*, said Adriaan. *It is as if you've done it before.* And his voice drowned in a gush of senses, swaying, sailing off shore. Pablo stood beside him, dressed, prescient, as if waving goodbye.

That morning, Maria Elena had kissed her husband's forehead. He was back early from his Tuesday night shift and seemed more himself today, collected, unlike he had been in a long time. So much with that man was a mystery to her; she had learned, however, to respect him and ferry his moods on her gentle soul to a calm shore. *Couples become a bit complacent and estranged after so many years together*, she told herself (and the one girlfriend she had in Oakland). She rarely ventured from the East Bay and never disturbed her husband at his trying job as a drug and alcohol counselor. Besides, English had never been easy to comprehend so she did not leave the neighborhood often. It took Maria Elena a great deal of courage to find out what Pablo was doing when he was not at home or at work those two nights each week. She would have never asked or investigated. There had been other women, she knew. Transient. Bodies that would provide the kinds of physical leisure that turns to dust under the covers after many years of cohabiting. Her dignity would had never allowed her to break Pablo's confidence in her and the precarious-but-permanent quality of their twenty years of marriage. Maria Elena was patient; through careful scanning of her husband's moods and silent words, she could flag the beginning and ends of his temporary escapades. After all that Pablo, the kids, and she had gone through—what could she do? The tough times settling in the U.S. when their kids were babies; Pablo's political affiliations; their sinister undertones; the dreadful and fragmentary memory of Chile. She once was a young housewife with almost no relatives, without much formal education. Nobody could tell much about her past. Nobody said much about anything at that time; it was scary and dangerous to speak. She had been conventional and Catholic, loyal in her own ways, careful, quiet, never letting the *diestra* hand know what the *siniestra* hand was doing. And it was, she knew this well, *sinister* indeed. She could see her husband's comings and going. If someone asked her what her husband did for a living, she had a shrug or a shy answer. But they had to go away in the middle of the night. It was Maria Elena's blind common sense, a muted and obstinate sense of survival, that pulled the family through the harsh times of settling in this foreign land. It was Maria Elena, the loyal woman behind her man, who had forged the reasons the family needed to hear, especially the children, and the stories that others expected from them, particularly at the beginning—the tale of young, exiled, fresh-faced immigrants with two lovely children. It was Maria Elena's pragmatism that made her remain calm, very calm, after she found out what she needed to know about Pablo's Tuesday and Thursday night shifts. It was her pragmatism that slipped the unfortunate little plastic bag into Pablo's hands and into Adriaan's veins.

There are pauses in even the worst of ordeals. Even the downtrodden and destitute sleep at some point, maybe at the break of dawn, when the street cleaner trucks try to sweep away the soot and trash of the City of San Francisco in an act of banal cosmetic surgery. At times Adriaan was able to stop meandering and sought shelter in a doorway, under cardboard and rags, in the arms of a fellow wanderer. There had been redemptions in Pablo and Maria Elena's lives: their children, for example. They had protected and overprotected them—from explanations and details of their past, from never going back to Chile, from never, ever conjuring any image that could in any way bring back the ghosts and their incessant chattering, the shattering of their long teeth, their withdrawal from pain as if from drugs, that incessant chattering of the long tooth that is killing them softly. Pablo and Maria Elena's children had been raised on a good American diet, with decent friends and associates, good schools and a future, deposits and savings for college, where they were now well poised to go; they would not be immigrants, exiles. Their little friends at school and the other parents had never asked too many questions because liberal people are trusting and sensitive and would never ask too much about this family that had been exiled under such horrific circumstances. Maria Elena and Pablo had forged ahead; they were stable; America is a good place to forge and forget, day-to-day. In their oasis, their menacing calm, Pablo had studied to get a decent job, and for a few hours he might have gone astray over the years, a brief fling here and there with a curious *gringa* who saw something exotic and spicy in his compact body, his soft manner, his shyness, his silent past—whatever it is that *gringas* delude themselves into thinking when they need to dress up their lust for a dark-skinned man. But two years ago, around the time Pablo was celebrating his twelfth anniversary at the Lookout detox center and he and Maria Elena were ignoring their twentieth anniversary of landing in the U.S., Pablo had changed. Maria Elena recognized the manifestations, something she had seen before, something to be aware of, at least for a while. One thing, however, was different this time. Pablo, on his Tuesday and Thursdays, was seeing a man, a young man.

A paroxysm of brilliant flickering light plunges across the room when released from the chamber where the Goliath drug has mixed with blood to galvanize the whole person, skinning him alive of his fear and his control and his training in good manners and decency and caution. Pablo had began to cook Adriaan's fixes the week that the young man said that he would go away: away from the sea; the city; the morning fog that was getting too dense; the miniature lives of those fags who sauntered through the Castro to their joyfully petty destinations; the earnest and tedious AIDS activists; the "A list" bodies enveloped in close-fitting Botoxed skins and speaking in fastidious mechanical voices on their fastidious cells. Adriaan was ready to depart now that Pablo seemed more in control of his life, less needy, more interested in getting back to the family he loved. However, those concoctions taken from Pablo's hands were making him crazy. They would take savage detours, a turn here, a turn there, move, moving, relentlessly in motion, his body contorting and not finding the comfort of gestures and postures. Their hours of quietude at the beginning and end of the evening, the appeasing and sensual food, their paused dialogue, and their lovemaking, all of it was getting lost in the hovering of Pablo over his face, telling him other things, new things, obscuring everything, making him run through tunnels and black out to wake up somewhere along Polk Street or deep in the Tenderloin. No more smiling and gentle greasy breakfasts at the Railroad Café, sipping coffee, catching up with his medicines, the little blue and green and red pills. Adriaan lost his job in three weeks; it was like a car accident, and Pablo seemed to be there, standing in the audience and watching him crash. (None of them saw Maria Elena that one night in which she crossed the Bay Bridge and searched for a name, a number, linked to a scrap of paper, perhaps a small square plastic bag she had found in his husband's pocket. He was, perhaps, intimately yearning to be found out.)

Watch and do nothing. Adriaan could not understand that Pablo would do nothing. Or he could not understand what Pablo was doing those days he came to see him, days that threaded seamlessly into one another and then snapped into knots, like his limbs and the compulsive rubbing of his steely tongue against his palate. Adriaan was unable to call (he might have picked up the phone and called the Lookout once, but he got the wrong number, and the soft voice of a middle-aged woman with a heavy accent responded, and he hung up). Adriaan was unable to use the computer, to shop for food until Pablo showed up again with another fix. Adriaan was unable to pause to ask...and maybe Pablo would... The last time he saw Pablo, Adriaan tried to collect his runaway thoughts and ask. Ask many things. Pablo seemed cold and distant and spat at him that he should try to get a hold of himself or he would end up in the Lookout, like the others. The rest of what was uttered that night was uncontrolled, contradictory, and terribly vindictive: *You know why I really ended up in this fucking country and stuck with freaks like you? Do you really want to know?* Adriaan's dilated blue gray eyes widened, he was bathing in his own sweat, tied spread-eagle across his bed, with bleeding nipples, bewildered hair, and drumming ears. Pablo had come all over him, like a small engine, after ramming up against him and swiftly maneuvering him down and binding him. *I had to come here because they betrayed me, after I had worked so hard for them. And what did they do? They protected the soldiers and the rich... They made me leave to protect someone else.* Pablo began to cry in anger. Adriaan watched him and asked: *Didn't you have to protect your family?* The look in Pablo's eyes stunned him. Pablo muttered, *You know how much I did to help that country, and this is how they paid me, erasing my past and my future for someone else's sake?* He beat his chest to prove his point. *I was the one who dragged out the truth kicking and screaming and pleading into the light of day. And I end up here with a...family, a...political-asylum claim, and a life sentence of pity from others.* Pablo's face drew nearer. *But nobody took the trouble to get to know me or ask me why I was doing it...I mean, the flaying and interrogating. The injections. The burning lips and pulled teeth.* Pablo kissed Adriaan's bitter mouth, and the young man showed no teeth, only lips, and kissed him back with great tenderness. Adriaan seemed to be whispering something, a light was lit inside his eyes, some understanding... *Nobody took the time? Your wife did, didn't she? And what did she find out? That you were worse than a red, a fag.* Pablo struck him across the face. *I bet she got busy plotting your future, that conniving bitch, she pussywhipped your fucking faggot ass all the way here, didn't she?* Pablo struck him hard across the face again, once, twice — until his eyes were swollen and he started to gag on his spit and blood. Mangled words stuttered out of Adriaan's mouth. *They took the trouble to get to know you, right? Those poor souls you tortured.* Pablo yelled, *I helped them speak their truth...many of them...and I took care of them afterward and they — believe me — they loved me — why can't you?* Adriaan's composure and Pablo's coming-undone were jarring. *You took care of them? How? Made them suck your hard little cock when they had no teeth left? You wanted to mess with their heads the way you mess with mine.* Before Adriaan could say anything else, Pablo used a long cloth, a sort of scarf, to gag him. *You are cruel and spoiled. You know nothing about fighting for your life and the life of others. What would you know when you offer your ass and your arms to whoever wants to take them? Look at you.* He slapped him hard, and poked him, and bruised him. *What I did was the reasonable thing to do under those circumstances.* For a moment Pablo was lost in a pool of memory, and it looked like he was going to get off the bed and walk out the door, but he turned back, swiftly. *They understood me and understood what I was doing. I was a good professional. I had a future. I didn't have to do any of that, but I thought I was being of service. And what did they do? Betrayed me. When they didn't need me anymore, they betrayed me — when they couldn't get away with political revenge anymore and the pressure from the outside was too much to handle.* Pablo was then kneeling next to Adriaan's body, one hand in the young man's gaping mouth and one hand pounding hard on his chest. *They deserted me.* A rib cracked. A light went out. Pablo ceased killing him softly for the night, knowing that Adriaan would not be able to understand or make sense of any more of his reasons, not for the time being. He was out of it. He knew that Adriaan would probably surface at the Lookout, looking for the gentle hands that cure and nourish so he could recover enough to be turned back loose into the streets and lose his mind again. *And now you want to leave me too. How could you? You, like me, someone with no future. We could have stayed together.* Pablo sat at the edge of the bed; his back slouched over as he put his shoes on with sluggish motions. *We could have stayed, together.* He stood up and left, leaving the door wide open behind him. Adriaan would be evicted anyway. He would not live there anymore. Adriaan sputtered something through his loosened teeth: *How could you?*

Francisco Ibáñez-Carrasco was born in Santiago de Chile in 1963 to an illiterate single mother who was a live-in maid. He grew up poor, the offspring of a military dictatorship, with an acquired taste for the bourgeoisie, boots, Catholicism, and queerness. In 1985, he disco-danced his happy-go-lucky feet to Vancouver, BC, where he promptly acquired his HIV, his Canadian citizenship (in 1991), his doctorate in Education from Simon Fraser University (in 1999), and an unending appetite for research, writing, and teaching. A sexual exile of sorts, he devotes many of his implausible tales to examining how desire geographically displaces individuals and infects lives. He lives, with his life partner John and ghosts of dead lovers and cats, in Vancouver, where he leads a double life as a decent social scientist and an indecent author. He exercises a polite degree of AIDS activism as the Co-Chair of the Canadian Working Group on HIV and Rehabilitation.